# PRAISE FOR *PHANT*

Mary Lynn Reed's *Phantom Advances* makes me yearn for the beginning stages of a terrible crush. There is so much desire in this collection—the need to be seen, touched—though her characters are most often watching, biding their time. And isn't this the best part? This is a remarkable collection, with clear precise prose and varied locales brought to life by her deft hand. I absolutely love these stories.
 —Mary Miller, author of *Biloxi* and *Always Happy Hour*

"I'd never considered *queer* a subject that could be studied or mastered," says a character in Mary Lynn Reed's spectacular story collection *Phantom Advances*. There is so much to love about this book—its slyly funny, brilliant characters, its roving, gimlet eye trained on the absurdist wonder of, say, the Ladies Bowling Tour in Kalamazoo, Michigan or the Conference on Algebraic Groups in Banff, Canada or a nudist gathering in Florida—but it's Reed's abiding interest in the slipperiness of identity, the fluid and haphazard dynamics of love and desire, and the way she heads, always, in the direction of generative and electrifying mystery that sets this singular collection apart.
 —Maud Casey, author of *City of Incurable Women*

Mary Lynn Reed's stories don't begin so much as erupt. Ten magic words—all she needs to put you in a new world, her world, where all the stuff in our world—the fights and kissing and desperation and loneliness—also happen, but in a new way. A way that creates urgent consequences for every minor detail. *Phantom Advances* happens everywhere in America, in corner bowling alleys and barber shops and off the grid motels everyone else forgot to notice. But there it is, the truth of all of us, hiding in plain sight, hiding in the journals in Reed's eye.
 —Barrett Warner, author of *Why Is It So Hard to Kill You?*

The protagonists in *Phantom Advances* push back against easy personal labels that will tidy up their loves, desires, and plans for the future. Often vulnerable and confused, they're nevertheless sturdy enough to know that life is not an equation and "identity" doesn't always solve for X. Mary Lynn Reed's psychologically acute stories celebrate the beauty and anguish of not knowing all the answers.
 —Pamela Erens, author of *The Virgins*

# PHANTOM ADVANCES

# PHANTOM ADVANCES

STORIES BY

MARY LYNN REED

Phantom Advances © 2023, Mary Lynn Reed

Published by Split/Lip Press
PO Box 27656
Ralston, NE 68127
www.splitlippress.com

ISBN: 978-1-952897-28-3

Cover and Book Design: David Wojciechowski
Cover Photo: Mary Lynn Reed
Editing: Pedro Ramírez

# CONTENTS

Acknowledgments

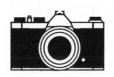

# LEAVING BOYSTOWN

Theo spun me around in the barber's chair, two fingers pressed against his lips. I'd asked for a "high and tight," and he didn't hold back. Displaying me like a prize, he announced: "Look at this amazing boy I've created!"

No one cared. This was Northalsted, Chicago. The place was full of smooth, real, beautiful boys. Through the mirror, I gave Theo my playful seductive glare. He fanned himself. "Jesus, Dean, have mercy on me—"

I shifted my legs.

Even with shoulder-length hair I was Sir'ed by the slightly distracted. No big deal. The second glances unnerved me, though. Upon catching the fullness of my chest, their demeanor turned to embarrassment, sometimes anger. There were still a lot of places where a girl with a crew cut could get her head bashed in.

Theo and I grew up together in Charleston. I crashed on his sofa my first term at Northwestern. Even after my advisor's promised funding came in, the proximity of Theo's sofa to the flashing lights and hard-throbbing techno of the Boystown club scene was hard to give up. Lesbian bars didn't do a thing for me.

"How's the love life?" I asked Theo.

He swept my shorn hair into a pile. "Richard studies too much. It'll be worth it when he's a doctor, I guess. Dustin is hot, *hot*—per usual. Keeps me sane."

"They still like each other?"

He winked. "This ain't South Carolina, darlin'. We in Boystown, and we like it!"

I was studying engineering back then. Had a knack for mechanical things. Dad was a tinkerer, Uncle Roy an electrician. I didn't know what I wanted to be but I was good at math and if I watched you take something apart, I could put it back together. Fast. Mom was hell-bent on my education. She had a little money tucked away that she never let Dad touch. So I went to Clemson, studied mechanical engineering. Far back as I remember, it was pre-determined I would leave Carolina, as if Mom always knew there was someplace else I ought to be. Grad school in a big, northern city seemed a fine alternative to an entry-level desk job in the hell-fire heat and blue-collar desperation of my childhood.

One night I was sipping warm beer out of a plastic cup at a campus party, found myself talking to Barb Wincheski, wife of Professor Peter Wincheski, chair of the department of electrical engineering. Barb owned an art gallery on Michigan Avenue. Her hands were well-manicured, nails painted bright pink. She knew how to blend with the college crowd. Her Chuck Taylors color-matched her turtleneck and blazer.

"I'm a bit of a shutterbug," I told her.

She raised an eyebrow. "Your look is striking. Ever do self-portraits?"

I fanned my exposed scalp. "I prefer looking at others. Behind the lens."

I visited her gallery. Took her to lunch. She loved the ballet, though she'd never danced.

"Pose for me," I said, and we wound up naked in my apartment, camera never coming out of the case.

Eventually, I did photograph Barb. Fully clothed, in her element. She hired me to take a series of candid shots on the opening night of a postmodern neoclassical exhibit that left me dizzy.

"What do you think?" she asked, delicately juggling a martini and her iPhone with one hand, grasping my arm with the other.

"I dig the symmetry," I said, enjoying the way she sidled in beside me.

"Anything else?" She took a long sip of the martini.

"Professor coming tonight?"

"He hates art." She slid swiftly back to her clientele.

I wasn't an event photographer, but I did my best. When I presented my selections to Barb she said I had a unique perspective.

"It's complex," she said. "What you focus on—where your eye lingers."

She wanted to see my independent work.

"What are the subjects you return to, again and again?" she asked.

"Underneath the El trains," I told her. "The shadows, steel. It's like an intricate geometric sky. I have hundreds of those shots."

We were on the futon in my apartment. She wore one of my large T-shirts and nothing else. I was in my boxers.

"Show me," she said.

I started a slideshow on my laptop.

She asked if I made my own prints, if I'd ever sold anything. I didn't hide my shock very well.

Her lips found my collarbone. "I have a buyer who will eat this up. I can sell your work. If you're interested."

And sell it she did. She had my images professionally printed and framed, sold five of them for five grand. I was in my Optimization of Engineering Design class when I got her text. The girl next to me reached out to make sure I was okay, that no one had died, or been in a car crash.

"No," I whispered. "My girlfriend is freakin' awesome."

That wasn't the only surprise Barb had in store.

"I'm leaving Peter," she said, over pink cocktails at The North End.

The DJ had just kicked up the volume and tempo, moving the bar's pace from Happy Hour to Evening Jam. I was so high on her sale of my photographs I almost missed what she said. Boys trickled onto the dance floor.

"I'm sorry, I think you said—"

"I'm leaving him," she said again.

"He's the Chair of the Department—"

Barb laughed. "And I'm the Queen of England. What the hell?"

"It was the first thing that popped into my mind," I said.

She downed her little pink cocktail and pulled me out to the floor. We danced until closing, then went back to my place and fucked until dawn.

Turned out Professor Wincheski's marriage had been on the skids long before I came to town. I still fell out of favor rather quickly in the department of electrical engineering. Professors gossip worse than teenage girls. It didn't take long for the faculty on the mechanical engineering side to begin looking at me askew as well. I hadn't exactly been blazing a trail to academic glory before I met Barb. I was holding my own. I could have made it to "Dr." if my energy had stayed focused in that direction.

As soon the divorce papers were served, I moved into Barb's apartment in the city. Bought a new camera with the money from that first sale and took an official leave of absence from Northwestern.

"I can't keep your funding on hold," my advisor said. "Grants don't work that way."

His office was full of textbooks and antique mechanical gadgets. The ridge in his forehead deepened with concern. He was a quiet man, spending his life surrounded by dusty, old things. It didn't have the magnetism of the crisp, clean lines in Barb's gallery downtown.

"It's a risk I want to take," I said.

Barb was smart and successful. She knew the art world, and she believed in me. I didn't know how to explain it to my professors, let alone my family back home in South Carolina. I went to see Theo before I turned the paperwork in. My gut wanted some back-up.

The barber shop was packed that day. So many gorgeous men, even I almost swooned when I walked in.

"You don't need me to tell you what to do," Theo said, dusting hair off a hunky blond's shoulders.

I tried to spin the stool I was on, but it wasn't a swivel.

"Tell me I'm not crazy," I said.

Theo raised an eyebrow. "Sweetheart, we both know you're crazy as hell."

I kicked at the base of the stool. I wanted that damn thing to spin.

"How's Dustin? Is he working?"

"He got a commercial!" Theo said. "Good pay."

Dustin did improv and stand-up comedy. He was always at an audition.

"It's not crazy to be a photographer, right? I don't have to be a gallery artist. I could get a job at the *Tribune*. Or the police department—I could shoot crime scenes."

"That's where your mind goes?" Theo said.

The blond in Theo's chair turned around. He was older than I'd thought. Forty or so. Must have been a bodybuilder at some point.

"You're too young for this much angst," he said. "If you want it, do it. Doesn't have to be your whole life. It's just the next thing on your list."

He had kind eyes. I smiled, said, "Thanks."

That first year with Barb was a frenzy of "new life." I explored the city with my camera, searching for just the right light to shoot my favorite spots. I took some classes. Film and darkroom techniques. Digital, too.

Barb also threw herself into a new passion: to be the best lesbian possible. She went to the Women & Children First bookstore, told the clerk: "I'm a late-blooming woman-loving-woman, and would like a reading list to get me up-to-speed." I found her eagerness to learn in this arena peculiar. There was a clinical aspect to her pursuit that caught me off-guard. I'd never considered *queer* a subject that could be studied or mastered.

One thing Barb missed from her Professor's Wife days were dinner parties. So one Saturday night we invited Theo, Richard, Dustin, and a lesbian couple Barb befriended at the gym over for homemade gnocchi and meatballs.

Lisa and Jamie Hunt-Waters were a Chicago power couple, for sure. Lawyer and financial analyst, respectively. Barb was an art dealer, after all, and wealthy friends made fantastic customers. I hadn't met Lisa and Jamie yet. Barb dressed me up in a white cotton button-down and a pair of leather wingtips for the evening. I went along without complaint. Didn't look half bad, actually.

Barb worked all afternoon on the gnocchi, a recipe she'd learned in Tuscany. "Cooking classes were the highlight of many vacations with the old Professor," Barb said.

"Worse things have come from marriage," Richard said, sneaking a taste of the sauce in the kitchen.

My contribution to the party was a playlist of downbeat ambient electronica, and twinkle lights I strung just under the crown molding throughout the dining room and den. Theo gave me a thumbs up on both, and the Hunt-Waters power couple didn't balk when they arrived, so I called it a success.

I passed around mini hors d'oeuvres.

Dustin and Theo chatted with finance-guru Jamie, who smiled a lot and didn't say much.

"What are you photographing these days, Dean?" Dustin asked.

"Train tracks," I said. "Intersections, in particular."

Richard swooped in. "Above ground?"

"No more under-shots of the El?" Theo asked. "Have you graduated from bottom to top?"

Dustin nudged Theo's arm. "Like you, dear—"

Theo feigned mock embarrassment, giggling.

"A-ha!" I said. "Tell me more—"

Jamie slipped away, looking uncomfortable, just as Barb tapped a silver fork against a crystal wine glass, and announced: "Dinner!"

Everyone settled into their places.

"What did I miss?" Barb asked.

"Dean was telling us about shooting train tracks," Theo said.

"Intersections," I said.

"Dean's work is progressing so rapidly," Barb said. "I can't wait to do a full show. It'll take Chicago by storm!"

"I'd love to see," Lisa, the lesbian lawyer, said. She was a firmly built woman with great posture. Clearly a gym fanatic.

Jamie was softer, a bit hunched. Contained within herself.

"You should give Lisa and Jamie a preview in your studio," Barb said. "After dinner."

My studio was a converted loft bedroom at the back of the apartment with a tricked-out computer and a massive monitor for touching up digital images. I didn't let anyone back there and Barb knew it.

"I've been reading this remarkable book," Barb said, wearing her 'polite company' smile.

Grateful for the change in subject, I grabbed a roll from the basket in the center of the table.

"It's a memoir of a female-to-male transsexual. Very thought-provoking," Barb said.

"See a lot of that in Boystown these days," Richard said, sipping his wine.

"Barb reads a lot of books," I said. "I think she's studying up for Queer Jeopardy."

Jamie smirked.

"I dated a drag queen once," Dustin said. "Hardest top I ever knew!"

Barb tossed her head to the side, directed her commentary toward Lisa. "The description of the writer's gender dysphoria—feeling out of sync with your own body—it got to me," she said. "Made me think hard about what it means to be a woman. Or a man."

"I think it's sad," Lisa said. "All the butches are disappearing, replaced by beards and hairy chests."

Richard touched his facial hair, and Lisa quickly added, "No offense."

"None taken."

"Besides that, there are so many different labels now. Non-binary, pan-sexual, omnisexual, an entire spectrum of asexuality. I can't keep up. Makes me feel so old," Lisa said.

"The gnocchi is really fantastic," I said. "Isn't it?"

Richard and Dustin moaned their agreement. Forks clanked against plates, scooping pasta with abandon.

"Richard's about to start an internship at Northwestern Memorial," I said.

Barb gripped the table. "Congratulations, Richard. That's wonderful," she said. "But Dean, I was talking about this book. About transsexuality. Why are you changing the subject? Does it make you uncomfortable?"

"No," I said. "Why would it?"

Theo laid his hand on my knee. I didn't realize my whole body had tensed into a tight coil until I flinched at his touch.

There was a decade's difference between my age and Barb's. I rarely thought about it until it lit up the room like a neon sign. She looked at me like a child.

"When did you stop using your girl name?" Barb continued. "When did you become Dean, and not Robin?"

The room fell quiet, except for the slow lounge groove still playing softly from the Bose.

I put my fork and knife down gently.

Theo jumped in, and said, "Eighth grade. We were thirteen and had just watched *Rebel Without A Cause*. I said, *I'm gonna call you Dean*. It just stuck. She was that cool. Then, and now."

Everyone's eyes were on me.

Barb had never mentioned this book or asked me these questions when we were alone. She waited until she had an audience. Until I couldn't deflect her interrogation. Little things that hadn't made any sense before became clear. She'd been carefully avoiding gendered pronouns for a while. When talking to her friends, she always referred to me as "Dean," never "she," "he," not even "them."

Barb stared at me across the long table. "So you found your true self at thirteen," she said. "Did your parents call you Dean after that?"

"My true self?" I said.

Theo, Richard, and Dustin sat very still, exchanging clenched-teeth glances.

"We're all unique," Jamie said, the sound of her voice startling everyone. She hadn't spoken more than a single word all night. Now she said, boldly, "Who we are. How we present ourselves to the world. Who and how we love. Can it be defined in a few words? Or given a proper name? We're just ourselves, I think. Labels limit us."

"Right," I said. "That's right."

"It's also about honesty," Barb said. "We should be honest about who we are, shouldn't we? At least to ourselves."

I was masculine, yes. Never felt comfortable in women's clothes. My voice was thick and heavy (sultry, some women said). My jaw was hard, square. What gives someone the right to take those facts and proclaim I'm not in the right body? Or that I'm not being honest about who I am? I was working myself up to say that out loud, when Richard cleared his throat, and stood up.

"I'm thirsty, that's what I am. More wine, anyone?" he said.

There was a collective exhale.

Barb got up to clear the dinner plates. I opened another bottle of wine. Two hours later, they were all gone. I sat in my studio with the lights out until the apartment was quiet.

I texted Theo to find out which club they'd gone to, then joined them in a sea of shirtless men. The sharp synthesized rhythm pulsed the back of my skull, left no room for worries, or questions. A hot, gay club was where it all made sense to me. Piercing female vocals soared above all the hard bodies, enveloped us like a maternal embrace. Sweat soaked through my sports bra, and I pulled my tank top off. Swung it lasso style, above my head. No one asking me who I was, or why I was there. We just danced. Stayed out on the floor for hours, bouncing away the night's tension until the blinding lights switched on at 4 a.m.

We ended up at the all-night diner.

Theo and Richard and Dustin. The three of them were as different as three gay men could be, yet together they worked. And they were smart enough not to dissect it or throw a lot of bullshit labels around to make other people comfortable.

"You okay?" Theo asked.

"Never better," I said, still drenched in sweat.

"Hang in there," Richard said. "I think that woman actually loves you. In her own, ex-professor's-wife-Michigan-Ave-art-dealer kind of way."

I laughed.

Dustin finished off a full stack of pancakes and two orders of bacon, then said, "Man, I wish we had some more of that gnocchi. That stuff was de-lish."

We spent another hour talking about Richard's internship and Dustin's commercial. Topics that would have made great dinner party conversation with the Hunt-Waters couple if Barb hadn't hijacked the night for her gender identity detective mission.

I bought some danish and coffee to go. At home, I put them on a little silver tray and brought it to the bedroom. Barb was sitting straight up, wide awake.

"Have fun with the boys?" she asked.

I placed the tray over her legs, kissed her forehead. "I brought you breakfast."

"Mmm-hmm." She moved the tray off the bed, pulled me down on top of her.

We moved together, slowly. Kissing. Rhythm picked up, and I reached

10

into the side-table.

"Why?" she said.

I stopped. "Why what?"

"Why wouldn't you answer my questions? Why were you so uncomfortable?"

I hovered above her. "Why'd you wait to ask in front of everyone?"

"I don't know. Maybe it freaks me out. Reading that book made me wonder. Whether you might be in some kind of gender crisis."

"Crisis? You know how that sounds, right?"

We moved apart, shifting to opposite sides of the bed.

"Do your parents call you Dean? Why don't I know the answer to that question? Have you ever talked to a therapist? If you won't talk to me—"

"Why does it matter what name my mom and dad call me? I like boys' clothes and I like to fuck women. So what? I don't need a goddamned shrink. Is this even about me?"

Barb sat on the side of the bed, head in her hands.

"Maybe you're in crisis," I continued. "Maybe you're not such a perfect *new lesbian* if I'm not a *real woman*? Is that it?"

"That's not it," she said, quickly.

"You said that awfully fast. Defensive?" I moved to the dresser, started shoving clothes into a duffle bag.

"That's not fair," she said. "I love you, you little shit. Can't you see I want you to be happy? This isn't about me. It's about you. I just want you to be honest with yourself—"

Outside of family, no woman had ever said she'd loved me before that. Leave it to Barb to declare it in the middle of a spat.

"I need to clear my head," I said. "I'm gonna go up to Evanston, get my Toyota out of storage, and take a drive."

"Where? Why do you need clothes? How long is this drive?"

I sat down beside her. Sighed.

"It took a while but yes, my parents do call me Dean. It's a nickname. That's all. I'm not in crisis. Whatever the hell that means. I'm just going to take a drive. I'll shoot wildflowers on the side of the road, and I'll think about what you're saying. Okay? I'll think about all of it. I just need to clear my head."

She sat up straighter. "Lisa texted me. She wants three of the pieces you showed her last night. You've got real talent, Dean. No matter what else happens, I can sell your work. Okay? Know that I will do that for you, no matter what."

· · ·

I stopped at the barber shop on my way out of town. Theo gave me a fresh cut and an extra-long hug. He walked me out to the car.

"I don't know about this back roads trip," he said. "There are a lot of Southern accents between here and Miami. What's wrong with the interstate? You like to drive fast."

"Everything's a blur from the highway. Barb's a pain in the ass but she might be right about a few things. If I'm going to be an artist, I should be more deliberate for a while. Too much of my short life has already been a blur. I should look closer, pay attention to the details—and maybe, understand more about myself."

Theo squeezed my hand. "Boystown to South Beach. It's a gay pilgrimage, baby…take me with you. I swear, I'll be very, very quiet."

I laughed, rolled the windows down in the Toyota. A pair of beautiful men holding hands passed by, smiling. I took a deep breath and headed south on Halsted.

# WHEN PERFECTION'S AT STAKE

The day after the pink envelope with the Ladies Professional Bowling Tour (LPBT) logo arrived in the mail, I got up early and headed to Piney Wood Bowl. My Uncle Dave owned the place, my father ran the Pro Shop, and I'd spent nearly every day of my twenty-one years in that loud, windowless hall. I liked the place best in the early morning, when it smelled like fresh oil from the lanes more than beer or shoe disinfectant, and you could hear the mechanics of the ball return operating clearly, with no kids yelling or pinball machines clanking in the background. In the morning, I left it dark, just the lights over lanes 49 and 50, where I practiced.

The letter from the LPBT welcomed me to join the Tour that fall, September 1982. It included a membership card with my name, Jossa B. Koller, printed double-size in all caps. There was a list of tour dates, locations, instructions for booking travel (bus lines, train schedules, a string of "official" Quality Inns), and a spiral-bound rule book I would read line-by-line every night between then and my first tournament in Kalamazoo.

Kalamazoo.

My dad came close in Kalamazoo once. He qualified for some pro events in the early 70s, went to the semi-finals a few times. He had a quirky hop-jump five-step approach that looked unnatural on a professional, but no one laughed at his 225 average. He'd started late, though, marrying and having kids instead of turning pro as a young man, and so he never got to the spotlight of Saturday afternoon TV. He still averaged 190 and shot a perfect game in a league every other year or so. Tendonitis slowed him down. He couldn't practice enough and his best days were memories now, he'd say. So he made a living drilling holes in rubber and plastic balls and giving lessons to kids who showed promise. Like me.

My father taught me the basic four-step approach at age six and I practiced for free at Piney Wood, as much as I wanted. By the time I was nine,
that meant every day. Coaching from Dad was always five minutes here or
five minutes there, textbook follow-through and ball placement. As I got
older, he threw in the occasional scolding when my temper flared and I lost
concentration. There wasn't a ball-return in all of Piney Wood Bowl's fifty
lanes I hadn't kicked in frustration after a 10-pin remained when it clearly
should have fallen.

At thirteen I was averaging 165, and Dad said it was time for a private
coach to elevate my game. My brother was three years older and a solid 180,
but he never caught the spark. There was no fire in his eyes, Dad said. We
didn't have much money and a private coach seemed extravagant. But Dad
insisted. You can't ignore talent and a gutsy determination, he said.

Darcy Inglewood was the best woman bowler in town, star of the Monday night Ladies' Scratch League, the City Invitational, and the Thursday
night High Rollers. She was powerful and strong, built like a middle-weight
boxer; her biceps flexed on her follow-through. She didn't have a fiery style.
I'd watched her roll near-perfect games, watched her win tournament after
tournament. She never lost her cool. I thought she lacked passion.

Dad said I was a hot-head with too much "passion" for my own good,
and Darcy was just what I needed.

It was 1974, and Darcy Inglewood sat at the scorer's table on lanes 49 and
50, her shiny black hair feathered and sprayed. She said, "Why don't you
throw a few?"

Strike, spare, another strike. She signaled me to stop.

"Where's your mark?" she asked.

"Outside."

I liked a dramatic finish. The big hook was my trademark. I always
played the outside line.

"Where exactly?" she asked. "Which board?"

She was kidding, right?

Her expression never changed.

My brother's voice carried down the concourse, yelling for Mom. At
least half my family was always at Piney Wood Bowl.

Darcy tapped the scoring table.

"Jos—sa—" She choked on my name, as if she were afraid of it.

I grabbed my towel, wiped my palms, held my right hand over the air
drier on the ball return.

"Which board?" Darcy repeated.

I grabbed for the resin bag, squeezed it between my thumb and middle fingers.

"I bowled a 247 last month," I said. "Couldn't miss that day."

"What was your mark then?"

"Outside," I said.

I picked up my ball and flicked my middle finger in and out of the plastic-gripped hole, echoing a crisp popping sound.

"Can I throw another?" I asked.

Darcy leaned forward. "When I won the invitational at Crestview two months ago I was hitting the eighth board on lane 42 for the first four frames. In the fifth frame I missed my mark, got lucky, found a better line on the sixth board by accident. Struck out the rest of the game on that lane playing that line. Lane 41 was tighter, smooth inside track on the fourteenth board. I rode it the whole first game of the finals."

She leaned back. "You want to hear about the second game? How 'bout the third?"

I propped the ball against my hip.

Darcy got up, walked over to her bag, took out a solid black ball, placed it on the return. She took out a pair of glistening gold-toed shoes, custom-made. Dad sold them in the Piney Wood Pro Shop.

"One game," she said. "You and me. The tenth board is our mark."

I hated her form. It was smooth, but dull. Rigidly consistent. No pizzazz.

Starting stance: ball held waist-high, elbows relaxed by her side. An easy, slow push-out in the first step, letting momentum take the ball over in the second. Arm fully extended into the third step, tight and straight, elbow locked and parallel to the floor, ball aligned with her head. Fourth step into slide, flowing silently to the release, follow-through precise.

Strike.

I stood behind the ball return, clutching my towel and resin bag.

Strike. Strike. Strike.

After four frames she stopped, pointed at me.

"Go," she said.

I took my position, stared ahead at the second diamond on the tenth board. There were forty boards on a lane, each one only an inch wide. I'd never aimed that precisely before. I was a cranker. I bowled on instinct, liked to leave everything loose, compensating for errors at the last minute. If I felt the shot going wide, I cranked it harder. If a shot felt tight, I could flatten it in the follow-through. I'd been bowling since I was four years old, and that was my style.

The lanes hadn't been oiled yet that day and they were finishing with a hard hook. I wanted to shoot farther outside than the tenth board. I needed that space for my curve on the back end. I made my usual adjustment, a half-step to the left and a slight twist of my hips to the right. Concentrating, I held the ball high, near my face, gripping it with my fingertips.

"Wait," Darcy said.

She was on the approach behind me.

I loosened my grip, ready to turn. Her hands touched my waist. Her warmth covered my back. She shifted my hips, faced me straight, then gripped my elbows with her palms and slid them down until the ball rested at my waist. She stepped around in front of me and continued to reposition my stance. She pulled back, and said, "Tenth board. Go."

I stood there for a minute, unable to push the ball forward and start the somatic responses. My brother was nearby. Uncle Dave shuffled around at the front desk.

No one could see what I felt. No one knew I was unable to move. I stood there, stiff at first then trembling, staring at my new mark. That one-inch piece of smooth lacquered wood was the only thing that existed. Finally, I found the will to push off and go. I focused so hard that I almost tripped over my own feet at the foul line. But I hit that tenth board perfectly. My hook wasn't as wide or as wild as I liked it, but the result was unforgettable. A dream strike. Pure and solid and loud.

Darcy was smiling. My game was forever changed.

I worked with Darcy every week for three years. I was averaging 210 at age sixteen, winning every tournament I entered. We met at Piney Wood Bowl every Friday afternoon at five. I bowled and she watched from the scorer's table. Sometimes she'd roll a few too, but mostly, she concentrated on me. She reined in the wildness of my game, helped sculpt and mold my natural talent into professional-level skill.

She never physically repositioned my stance again. She talked me through it with her hands in her pockets, barking out code phrases I grew to loathe.

"At your waist," she'd say, when I held the ball too high.

"Natural grip," she'd say, when I cocked my wrist into a cranking position.

I listened, but I didn't become a Darcy Inglewood clone. I had too much "personal flare" for that, Dad said. My game was my own.

We were separate. Coach and student.

For every minute I spent practicing and bowling in leagues and competitions, I spent five more aching to be older, aching to be more to Darcy than just a kid with a bad temper and a naturally wild hook. I longed to ride in her dented Subaru or eat supper in her cramped two-room apartment I'd never seen. I spent my entire teenage existence wanting her, and yet I barely knew anything about her. The boundaries between us were silent but solid. She wasn't married. She didn't talk about boyfriends or girlfriends. I was never even sure which one she'd prefer. She worked a boring nine-to-five doing the books for a window-and-door installation company, and she bowled every night. As far as I could tell, that was all there was to know. But before I'd ever dated, or held hands, or kissed anyone, I imagined a life shared with Darcy. A life where I knew her completely, and she knew me.

When I was seventeen and Darcy was twenty-seven, I went to college and she left to join The Tour. I majored in business, made C's, spent too much time at the bowling alley, sharpening my game.

I dated a couple of guys in college. None of them held my attention past a few athletic sexual romps. I had a roommate for about a year who was stuck in a free love time warp. She brought home a steady stream of men and women, sometimes several at once. She tried to convince me I should "expand my horizons." I kept my head in my books, pretended not to understand—or to care—what she meant. I worried I should make some kind of effort in that direction but my energy just wasn't there.

By the time the big pink envelope came from the Ladies Professional Bowling Tour, I was back living at home, bowling twelve hours a day, mostly on lanes 49 and 50 at the Piney Wood Bowl. And every time I closed my eyes on that familiar approach, I saw Darcy Inglewood. At the scoring table. Standing beside me. I felt her hands on my waist. The touch she gave, the one she took away.

I arrived in Kalamazoo with one suitcase of clothes and nine bowling balls. During qualifying rounds, I was paired with three other rookies, two bouncy girls with thick southern accents and Lucia Simmons from New York, who talked like a construction worker and looked more uncomfortable bowling in a skirt than I thought my brother would. Skirts were required on The Tour and I'd been practicing in one for three years to prepare.

Lucia was a lefty with a temper. I liked her immediately. After missing a 5-10 split pick-up in the second game, she kicked the ball return and knocked the hard plastic shell off. The LPBT officials conferred, then gave her a ticket: one more outburst and she'd be gone.

Flare ups like that didn't plague me anymore. I wasn't cold or dispassionate, but I knew how to contain myself on the lanes.

After two days of qualifying at Kalamazoo, I was in 23rd place, just ahead of Lucia. Only twenty-four bowlers would qualify. Lucia asked if I wanted to grab dinner at a spaghetti place in town. I was hesitant. After she confirmed the place wasn't too expensive, I agreed. Even the solid pros barely got by on their winnings.

The restaurant had a romantic atmosphere that surprised me. I was in jeans, cowboy boots, and a cardigan; Lucia wore a blouse and her bowling skirt, said she needed to get used to sitting in the damn things.

We got a booth near the back and Lucia ordered a bottle of red wine. I said I didn't want any, but the waiter brought two glasses and filled them up so I sipped the wine and tried to read the menu in the dimly lit corner.

"Nice, isn't it?" Lucia said.

We talked about our families, about bowling. Lucia was sweet, attentive, trying to flirt. My mind wandered.

She reached across the table for my hand, and I pulled away. That's when I saw the four of them. Nikki, Tish, Donna, and Darcy. At a big round table in the center of the room, eating appetizers and laughing.

Darcy wore gold hoop earrings. Her smile was wide; she looked relaxed. All those years of coaching me, she had been so guarded, reserved. She'd been holding herself back.

"The big names," Lucia said, looking over.

For a butch girl from Brooklyn, Lucia was surprisingly gossipy. "Guess who—" she said. Even the straightest-looking stars with husbands and kids at home, Lucia had stories about. I didn't believe half of the pairings, and mostly I didn't care. But I was happy she didn't have anything sordid to report about Darcy. Even as I dreamed of being with her myself, I hoped Darcy was above the fray of all that distraction. Darcy and I—we were beyond that. In my mind, at least.

I caught Darcy's eye as she scanned the room. I had an urge to run to her, throw my arms around her neck, and say, "Darcy, I'm here. I'm twenty-one!"

I grabbed a piece of garlic bread instead.

Ten minutes later, Darcy stood at the edge of our table.

"Jossa Koller. I heard you were one of us now. Congratulations."

Lucia gazed at her, awe-struck.

"Thanks," I said. "I'm 23rd in the qualifiers."

Darcy smiled, and I clutched my napkin. "Good luck tomorrow, then." She touched my shoulder, squeezed it gently. "Can't wait to see you out there."

The next day I qualified and Lucia didn't. She shook my hand when the round was over, wished me luck with the big names. Grasping my arm, she pulled me close enough to whisper.

"Be careful," she said. "Some of them will do anything—and I mean *anything*—to win."

She arched her eyebrows.

"Okay—" I said.

In the semi-finals, I was paired with Josephine Lowell from Oklahoma, and on the lanes directly next to us were Darcy and Nikki G. I'd seen Nikki on TV so many times, her style so seductively smooth. She and Darcy joked and nudged each other before the competition began. When the score-keeping kicked in, they turned stone-faced and serious. Erecting walls of mental toughness, concentration, they barely acknowledged one another.

I tried to ignore them and Josephine Lowell too. Focused on throwing strikes, keeping my head down. Two games in, I was down twenty pins. The lanes were tough. Notched up a level in difficulty from the qualifying round. Oil spread uneven and tapered off near the heads. I needed a solid game to finish the round or I'd be out. I changed balls and tried to stop myself from glancing at Darcy in between frames.

I started the third game with four strikes. Then another. Another. When I made the seventh, attention shifted away from the big names and over to me.

Who was the new girl tracking down a perfect game?

In the eighth frame, I took an extra breath as I held my stance; Darcy and Nikki paused to watch, and so did the pair on the other side. An eerie quietness settled in. I missed my mark by a board, but luck and spinning momentum compensated and all ten pins fell. Polite applause from the neighboring lanes. I managed a weak smile. Darcy was only three steps away, angling toward me. I grabbed my towel off the return as her warm hand landed on my shoulder.

"Breathe," she said in my ear.

I sat down. Inhaled. Exhaled.

Josephine finished her spare.

Ninth frame. This time the silencing effect pushed out beyond our neighboring lanes. Four, six, eight lanes on either side paused: the game's customary politeness when perfection's at stake.

Standing in my start position, my mind jumped back to Darcy's hand on my shoulder. Flashing, spiraling through eight years time.

I'm thirteen again. Darcy's hands on my waist, repositioning my hips, her palms on my elbows, adjusting my position. My awakening was forever tied to the definition of my bowling stance.

I stood still for too long and when I finally pushed off, my bicep clenched and I tugged, arcing my natural swing wide. Overcompensating, I cranked it like a wind-up toy. It felt horrible. The worst ball I'd thrown in five years. But somehow, miraculously, it landed right on the mark and hooked into the pocket.

Strike!

I exhaled and dropped my head into my hands as the last pin fell. More applause. Shouts of "Go get 'em, girl" and "Way to go, kid" from the tour vets. Lucia stood with a group in the back. She gave me a goofy thumbs up; it made me laugh. A welcome relief from the tension.

Darcy pushed in close again. It happened so fast it almost seemed natural. She held her hand out toward me, palm up, and wiggled her fingers, playfully.

"Gimme some of that," she said.

I stared at her fingers as the terrazzo floors beneath me turned to quicksand. It didn't make sense. It was a common sight for an amateur league, or during junior handicap play. A teammate's transfer of luck, hot fingers to cold.

But I wasn't a kid in a league. This wasn't a practice round. I was a professional, and this was my debut. Pros don't steal one another's luck during competition. It just isn't done.

My face went hot. Temper rose so fast, I was boiling. *Don't break the flow*, Darcy'd always told me. *Don't let anyone distract you when your game is on.* This was my moment. Three strikes away from perfection in my first Tour event. I stared at the terrazzo under my feet and didn't offer her my hand.

Darcy slipped her hands into her pockets and for a moment, she looked ashamed.

I tried to conjure rivers flowing, sunsets reddening, quiet moments by a fireplace. I couldn't shake the thought of Darcy's hand reaching out for mine, a flash of near desperation in her eyes.

All those years I'd wanted her hands on me. Wanting more from her. Feeling so alone, all the time.

I turned back to Lucia. She was biting her fingernail, clenching her teeth.

I would not look at Darcy again.

The first strike in the tenth frame came easy. Quick. Growing enthusiastic applause; respect rose on my new colleagues' faces, slight trepidation in a few. Who was this new kid? How far will she go?

When I stood up again, all the lanes were silent. The whole place stopped. There was a real chance at perfection for a Tour rookie. I tried not to think too much, but I'd only been there once before. Shot a 298 when I was eighteen. Left the 7-10 split on the final shot. I'd never actually reached perfection. So I savored the moment. Thought about my dad and his perfect games. His fleeting moments on the men's tour. I thought about lanes 49 and 50 at the Piney Wood Bowl. So many hours practicing.

Darcy.

No, I told myself. *Focus.*

I began to move, and the approach felt smooth. Nothing distracted me. I held my form; I hit my mark, consistent with the others, but the ball hit the pocket weak. Ten-pin ringer.

One solid lonely pin standing in the corner.

Disappointed sighs rippled through the crowd and noise quickly returned to the lanes. Everyone waiting out of politeness now went back to their own games. I sighed and picked up the spare without effort. Final score: 289. Not even close to perfection.

How unforgiving, the game I loved.


I survived until the next day's round, when I fell out without fanfare. Darcy was twelve lanes away. After a weak start, she was back on track to make the TV finals. She glanced my way a few times, didn't approach.

Lucia bought me dinner that night at the same spaghetti place. Over coffee and cheesecake she told me about her first and only near-perfect game. As she talked, the tension in my shoulders lessened.

Lucia was a gentle, sweet lover. I feared that someday I would be the cold, elusive girl whose heart she never truly won. I wasn't proud of that, or of the ruthless, hard way I felt when Darcy stared at the two of us together. When I watched Darcy closely, waiting for her perfect form to falter, just a little, or her concentration to slip.

Darcy and I didn't become enemies on The Tour. Not friends either. We were just two professionals. Seasoned vet and rookie.

And when I wrapped myself tightly around Lucia's warm body at night, I held on for as long as I could, replaying the day's games, frame by frame, board by board, hearing Darcy's voice in my ear, saying, "Gimme some of that," with her hand extended, desperately waiting to be touched.

# THE BEAUTY INSIDE

The first speaker wrote his tiny symbols and Greek letters on the chalkboard, each stroke heavy with precision. I'd read all of his papers, yet I had never imagined the mathematician behind those ideas occupying a body at all, much less the soft, stooping, round one at the front of the room, holding the crowd in rapture.

I tapped my toe on the concrete floor and scanned the hall, counting other women. Five, in addition to me.

My cuticles tasted bitter.

Three weeks in the Canadian Rockies. The brochure for the International Conference on Algebraic Groups featured white-capped mountains, promising a tour up the Icefields Parkway and a chance to mingle with the world's most famous algebraic geometers.

I'd never seen a glacier.

The old guy next to me looked down at my foot. My tapping shook the seat row.

"Sorry," I said, but the tapping kept on.

"Inspiration awaits you in Banff," my thesis advisor had said. "No distractions."

*Finish the proof*, he meant.

Two thousand miles from Ann Arbor, I would breathe the mountain air, photograph the glaciers, and forget about Sylvia Cortez. She didn't exist. Her husband didn't either. The restraining order against me was immaterial.

I opened my notebook and turned the page. My unfinished proof lay in ruins. I tuned out the speaker and his tiny, heavy hand, and began to work.

At check-in the night before, a pale guy wearing a tangerine headband recited a list of rules. The Banff Centre was part conference facility, part artists' colony. Artists were "residents," conference attendees were visitors. Visitor privileges were limited.

*Heed all posted signs.*
*Don't disturb residents at work.*
*Don't trespass where trespassing isn't allowed.*
*Beware of the elk, aggressive if threatened.*
*Enjoy your stay.*

After the morning session, I went back to my room and grabbed my camera. My eyes could barely keep up. Steep mountain ridges. Endless sky. Distance impossible to judge. Blood-rich crimson flowers flooded the foreground. I pushed beyond the conference facility toward the colony where artists slipped ghostlike in and out of huts and halls.

Mozart spilled out of the music building, followed by a deep French-accented voice. I snuck inside, wondering whether I could blend among the artists. The source of the music was a young woman around my age, straight black hair to her waist. Her hands arced briskly on piano keys. I concealed myself behind the studio door. The teacher clapped once and the woman stopped playing. My sneakers squeaked.

"Artists only!" the man with the deep voice yelled.

There was no time to concoct a convincing lie, so I ran. When I looked back, the woman stood at the studio threshold, smirking.

I met Sylvia Cortez my first year at Ann Arbor. She was a philosopher, a grad student like me. She wasn't brilliant or beautiful, but she could talk for hours about epistemology and existentialism. None of it made sense to me but I listened; I got as close to her as I could. Her husband was a chemist, a full professor twenty-five years older. I never understand what young women see in old men. Love, why it inflicts itself on us when it does, can never be understood.

Sylvia called me exotic, passionate, a genius. She'd never met a woman as fascinating as me. I bristled at "woman." Recoiled from the label "girl-friend." I lived in my head, inside an abstract world void of gender and physical sensation.

Until Sylvia said she loved me.

At dinner, I picked at my new potatoes and string beans, trying to ignore the conference chitchat. Name-dropping of theorems and collaborators, boasting of journal publications and colloquia invitations. A graduate student from Oregon sat down next to me, tried to make conversation about the abysmal state of the academic job market. I smiled, rose, escaped.

I found myself browsing magazines at the market shop. Wrought iron chairs scraped the concrete; voices grew closer. A man and a woman, her clothes mostly black, his shirt paint-stained a glowing chartreuse. I nodded at them, and Neon Shirt said, "Join us?"

"No, thanks," I said.

"What's your name?"

I put down my magazine. "Lane," I said.

He turned to the woman. "Didn't you date a chick named Street once?"

"Yes," she replied, curling her upper lip.

I looked at her and she scanned me: up, down.

"Come on, sit with us," the man said, pulling out a chair.

"I'm a conference guest. A mathematician. Not an artist."

The woman tapped the chair with her fingernail.

They quizzed me on logical paradoxes and special relativity, two things I knew embarrassingly little about. Vince was a thirty-year-old painter who looked nineteen. Olga, a poet. She used freakishly rare words, and when she thought hard about something, she clucked her tongue against the roof of her generous mouth.

Vince said he wanted to paint me, called my boyish features "striking," my sleepy brown eyes seductive. I laughed and tried not to look at Olga.

When the market shop closed, Vince took me aside, said he needed to know: him or Olga, which did I prefer?

"Is that a general question, or a specific one?"

He smiled. "I dig the androgyny," he said. "Just so you know."

Over his shoulder, I saw the pianist approach, marching like a soldier. "You know *her*?" I asked.

"Ah—Glacier Girl—"

She walked past, never looking up.

"I heard her play," I said.

"She's brilliant. But she doesn't speak to mortals."

I searched the horizon. She was gone.

"So, not Olga, not me. But Glacier Girl—"

I dug my fists into my back pockets, rocked myself. "I came here for the glaciers."

The speaker the next morning was one of the female mathematicians, a full professor from New Delhi in a purple print sari. The rhythmic highs and lows of her accent pushed me into a Zen-like space. I worked on my proof, slipping in and out of calculations like caves, deep tunnels of concentration.

I skipped lunch. Banff bustled with high-season cacophony: bus engines rumbling, couples arguing, tour guides competing for attention. I made my way through town, crossed the Bow River, found a winding trail near a light covering of brush. Standing at the river's edge, I shot the curve of water flowing, the snow-capped mountains beyond. Tried not to think about Sylvia.

Up the riverside trail was a slight incline, a grassy lawn. As I rounded a bank of evergreens, two elk appeared, one large and antlered, the other smaller, female. I waited. The antlered one lifted his head. I raised my camera and focused. The female darted off, while the male stood there posing.

I wandered back into town and found a coffee shop at the edge of the hotel strip. As I searched for a menu, a small voice behind me said, "Hello."

Startled, I bumped the counter. Grabbed the stack of menus before they fell on the pianist's head.

"Didn't mean to scare you," she said.

I clutched my camera bag.

"You a photographer?"

I opened my mouth but no words emerged.

She shrugged, went back to her coffee.

"Have you eaten?" This I blurted out, like an ill-mannered child.

She squinted behind a large mug, her eyes lined dark with mascara.

I extended my hand, "I'm Lane."

She didn't respond.

"I was on the trail by the river. The elk come right up to you. The males, at least. They're desperate to be caught on film. Not the females. Very skittish. I missed dinner at the Centre. I'm a mathematician. I hate mathematicians."

Finally, she smiled.

"I'm Taylor." She put her coffee cup down. "I hate musicians and artists."

I felt my face flush.

She knew of a diner so we went there. She wouldn't talk about music. I wouldn't talk about math. That was the deal.

"Why do you come to the Centre if you hate other artists?" I asked.

She leaned forward. "Have you seen the glaciers?"

"Not yet."

Her eyes were light green and enormous. She squeezed her fingers together as she spoke. "You expect pure whiteness, right? But they're blue.

Blue ice hanging off a mountain. The lakes look radioactive. The minerals make everything glow: turquoise, chartreuse. It's other-worldly. I come here every summer I can. For the glaciers more than the colony. Seeing them once in a lifetime is *not* enough."

She tapped my camera bag. "Be sure to look with your eyes though, not just your lens. Tourists miss everything trying to grab the perfect photo." She took a deep breath. "You have to hold the beauty inside. Let it fill you up. It won't fit in a picture."

I took a bite of my burger and studied the shadows on her face. The fluorescent lights in the diner tinted her pale skin slightly blue.

"I know what they call me," she said. "They think I'm obsessed with the Icefield. Or maybe they think I'm a bitch. Ha! I don't care. They're boring. And so full of themselves. I really can't stand artists."

I nodded, sorry for the enormous amount of food I'd just forced into my mouth. I covered my face with my napkin, chewed faster.

"Vince try to fuck you yet?" she asked.

I choked, tried to swallow without gagging.

"Sorry—I forget how to talk to people," she said.

I cleared my throat, took a long sip of water. "He said you didn't speak."

She laughed. "Not to him."

We walked back to the Centre. When we approached the artists' colony, Taylor slowed. I felt her tension reemerge as we neared the residence.

"I'm giving a recital," she said. "You could come if you want."

"Great!"

"You don't have to."

"What day? Time?"

"Look for the signs," she said, then disappeared behind an evergreen.

When I got back to the dorm, two mathematicians sat in the outer lobby, arguing about the higher cohomology of sheaves.

"That's it! It vanishes!" the younger one said, gesticulating.

The older man leaned in, enthralled. They looked like lovers.

Thoughts of Sylvia rushed through me for the first time in hours.

It was late but the sky was still aglow and hazy. Prolonged northern dusk. I craned my head out my room's window, heard soft footsteps, twigs breaking. From behind a bank of trees came an elk, no antlers. A few feet from my window, her gaze locked with mine. I eased back, tried not to scare her. Listened to her breathe.

• • •

I slept in and skipped the morning session. At lunch, two guys in the cafeteria were shouting in Russian. The woman from Oregon stepped in line behind me with a plastic tray.

"What's going on?" I asked.

"Thorbeau and Krauss discovered a new cohomology theory last night. The Russians were working on something similar. They've been scooped. Isn't it awesome to be here?"

I grunted acknowledgment, ordered macaroni and cheese. Took a seat by the window and opened my notebook. The grad student from Oregon fell in with the others.

Math buzzed through the room in a half-dozen languages, creating a brilliant white noise against which I ate my mac and cheese, thought about the glaciers and Taylor's green eyes.

I put my tray on the conveyor belt and went to the market shop. Olga and Vince were there, lurking by the magazines.

I felt a strange craving for the clove cigarettes displayed behind the counter, though I didn't smoke.

"Look at her," Olga said. "Soulful. Seductive."

Vince tugged at my sleeve. "I must paint you soon."

*Why are you here*, I wanted to ask them. *Why are you talking to me?*

Over Vince's shoulder, I saw Taylor approaching again. Her gait was sharp and determined, like a conductor stabbing the beat forward.

I moved toward her and said, "You disappeared last night."

Vince whispered something to Olga. Taylor watched them.

"I have to practice," she said, pushing past me.

I ran after her and grabbed her arm. She looked at my hand and her expression sent a shiver through me. She pointed toward the music building. "Don't lurk outside my studio today."

"I'm not a stalker."

"Who said I cared if you were? Just not today. I need to focus."

I thought she was going to leave, but she sat down on a bench and folded her arms across her chest.

"Were you looking for me just now?" I asked.

She shrugged. "Are you any good at math?"

"Of course. I wouldn't be here if I wasn't." I sat down next to her. "Can't do much else, actually."

"You like it then. It gives you pleasure."

"It bores me. I loved it once—I must have. But when I try to focus now, I can't. It's like I've gone too far, but also not far enough. I'm stuck."

Her shoulders dropped and I leaned in. For a second, I thought I could do anything. Reach out and hold her hand or touch the side of her face. But I sat still. Her green eyes glistened in the sun. She stood and said, "Recital's tomorrow night at seven."

As she moved past me, her fingertips brushed my shoulder. At the music building door, she waved.

I made love to Sylvia once in the dark woods behind her house, on an old Army blanket I'd bought at Ranger Surplus. It was a scratchy brown wool that made my knees raw. After she came, she left me there alone, sweat-cold and shaking under falling autumn leaves. I watched her window for hours. Shadows moving behind the curtains. She wasn't alone, but I was. With dead leaves burrowed in my clothes and the smell of her on my skin, I sat there, unable to make myself go.

I spent the afternoon on a bench at the far edge of the Centre's campus, retracing my unfinished proof. Absorbing every line, verifying the purity of its truth. Digging for flaws and new insight. When I looked up, three female elk stood across the lawn, grazing. A fourth appeared. They didn't seem to notice me.

I reached into my camera bag.

"Hey!" A gruff male voice approached.

The elk ran off.

Vince slapped me on the back.

"They were very close," I said. "It would have been a great shot."

"They're like rodents around here, you know." He picked up my notepad. "You don't seem like the math type to me. Who are you, really?"

I shrugged. "I don't know. Who the hell are you?"

He laughed. "I've got some time now. I'll show you who I am, if you're ready to pose." He threw a few fake boxing jabs at my face. "So serious," he said. "Come on."

Light spilled through high windows into Vince's studio. He pulled a stool out, asked if I wanted a beer. His paintings were neatly stacked against the wall.

"I'm not getting naked for you," I said.

He snapped his fingers. One, two, three times. "Close your eyes," he said.

He began to whistle. I felt his hand touch my foot. "Keep 'em closed—" he said.

He spun me around on the stool.

Bold crimson background, pale-skin subject. Taylor, naked on a glowing bed of green. A chaise longue. Her eyes painted the same radioactive chartreuse. Vince's neon shirt.

"There's more," he said, lifting up the next one.

Taylor and Vince, their bare limbs entwined under a zebra-print throw. The two of them crouched atop the chaise longue, flowing down a river of rapids, glacier-ice blue.

"She was a wild time," he said. "Brief. But hot, that Glacier Girl. Until she's through with you."

When I was eleven I ran away from home, certain things would be better "out there." I was impatient: I wanted everything to go faster, to see everything sooner. I consumed math and science like water, but they were too easy for me. I preferred literature, art, sports. Things I had so little talent for it was pointless to try. But those were the things I wanted.

*If I could just get away*, I thought. *Be anywhere except inside my own skin. As a child. As a grown-up. "Out there," things will be better. Out there I will create something, capture something, be something.*

*And someone will see it. Someone will know.*

The next day the conference transformed. The original schedule was suspended and Thorbeau and Krauss took the floor, laying out their new theory, highlighting open research questions.

The graduate student from Oregon sat down next to me.

"What an opportunity," she said. "To be here, right now."

Dizzy from lack of sleep, I forced myself to copy down Thorbeau's list of problems like a scribe, a mathematical monk. I looked at the woman: braided blond hair, sleeveless print dress, Birkenstocks.

"I'm Judy Rinaldi," she said. "We haven't really met."

I looked away.

"The inner alcove question is fascinating," she said. "All that intricate geometry removed from the algebraic formalism. Are you into that?"

I capped my pen, shut my notebook.

At the market store I gave in to the clove cigarettes I'd been coveting, and a sketchpad too. In my room, I smoked and scribbled, studied the brochure for the Icefield tour.

Just before seven, I splashed water on my face then sprinted to the music hall. I took a seat in the back, tried to catch my breath.

Vince gripped my shoulder. "There's an empty in the front row."

I got up and took the seat in the front. When Taylor walked onto the stage, everything turned crimson. I blinked into the blood-red spotlight and she was naked, wrapped around Vince's torso. I shook my head, tried to fight the image off.

She began to play.

I focused on her fingers. The way they flowed on and off the keys, over and under each other. Mozart's Sonata No. 18 moved through me like a narcotic, thick and hot and inescapable. The mood shifted in the second piece. A reticence. Taylor's expression turned calculating. Beethoven, the Hammerklavier, piercing and clean.

When she left the stage she kept her head down, oblivious to the applause. I went outside, paced, smoked, watched the crowd disperse. Olga watched me from across the lawn.

Back inside, the hall was empty and quiet.

Taylor appeared in the shadows. "The Beethoven was no good."

I fumbled with the cigarettes. She grabbed the pack from me, tossed it on the floor.

"I said, the Beethoven was no good."

I had no idea what to say to her.

"Vince showed me his paintings."

She sighed. "He shows everyone. They're pretty good, actually." She leaned toward me. Her eyes glowed.

She kissed me.

*Crimson red, glacier-ice blue.* Free-falling, I wrapped my arms around her, pulled her closer.

She pushed me away, and said, "I have to go."

My fingers tightened their grip. "Why'd you do that? Why does this happen to me?"

We struggled. I tried to kiss her, softly.

She dug her fingernails into my forearms and yelled, "Stop!"

I tucked my thesis at the bottom of my suitcase. My proof, unfinished. I bought more film at the market store. More sketchpads, clove cigarettes. I didn't see any of the mathematicians again until the day of the bus tour up the Icefields Parkway, the conference-sponsored glacier trip.

I told the organizer my name and he searched his list. Although he didn't recognize me, he reluctantly let me board the bus. The others clumped together in groups. The woman from Oregon sat with Thorbeau and Krauss; she carried a bag full of pre-prints, talked briskly of schemes, sheaves, alcoves.

I pressed my forehead against the cold bus window, focused on the tour guide's narration.

Bow Lake and Crowfoot Glacier. Valley of the Ten Peaks. The vistas dwarfed everything.

At Lake Louise, a group of mathematicians stayed on the bus. They'd been working the entire time. I tried to ignore them, wished I didn't understand what they were saying. The new mathematical structure they were navigating was fragile. Intricate. They were threading it together, making it whole.

I walked down to the lake. Cloudless blue sky above, mountain ridge and evergreen forest beyond. The rolling rhythm of the bus and the nonstop cackle of the mathematicians working had disoriented me. I felt queasy and my chest ached.

When I returned to the bus, the tour guide was silent. His narration of roadside wildlife and centuries of natural history had ceased. I looked around, confused. The organizer was thanking him.

"I know it's an unusual request," he said. "There's a group in the back working on a remarkable theorem. The silence will really help their concentration."

The tour guide waved him off, said, "No problem."

I gripped the seat in front of me. "What did you say?"

"They're working," the organizer said.

"So you stopped the guided tour?"

He nodded.

The bus driver watched me through the rearview.

"Why did we come here?" I yelled. "Why come to one of the most beautiful places in the world, if not to experience it? We only have one day!"

I stood up, looked around at the rest of them. "What kind of people are you? Do you not see what's out your window? It's right there. How can you ignore it?"

Seventy-five mathematicians glared at me.

"Mathematics is beautiful too," the organizer said, calmly. "It waits in our collective mind. We are responsible for breathing its beauty into the world. How can you call yourself a mathematician and not see *that*?"

The bus stopped and the tour guide called out: "Peyto Lake."

I got off the bus. At the look-out vista, I was alone. I gripped my camera. The lake glimmered phosphorescent turquoise. Like nothing I'd ever seen.

I snapped a picture. Another.

Then, through the tiny frame of my viewfinder, Sylvia appeared. Stretched out on blue satin sheets. Her husband on top of her. He was old, flabby, balding, but she clung to him. Pressed herself hard against him. She loved him.

And I was at their bedroom window.

I snapped another picture.

The organizer was waiting outside the bus to tell me they were cutting the tour short.

"You're right," he said, glancing around. "The glaciers are magnificent. But we'll have to see them another time. Krauss and Rinaldi have just proved a new theorem. If we turn back now, there's still time for one more lecture tonight. They can clean up the loose ends before everyone leaves tomorrow. Everyone agrees it's the right way to end such an extraordinary event."

I looked north up the lonely highway. The Columbia Icefield was fifty miles away.

"I want to see the Icefield," I said.

"Sorry," he said. "We're going back to Banff."

Back in my seat, I gritted my teeth and closed my eyes.

There is no satisfactory definition of beauty. No absolute understanding of its essence.

I tried to conjure a pure moment of Taylor playing Mozart. Tried to remember the last time I was in an art museum.

Soon I was adrift in a phantom memory from first-year abstract algebra. Galois theory. Richly seductive mathematics from such simple beginnings, a basic desire to understand polygons and polynomials. From that, intricate abstraction and discovery, connections between apparently disparate structures. The result: dissonant forms woven together, forever, in rich lattice arrangements.

Like ice crystals of truth.

I checked out of the Banff Centre as soon as we returned. Cancelled my flight to Ann Arbor.

"When should I book your new return?" the airline operator asked.

"Cancel it," I said. "No return."

I checked into a small motel near the diner where Taylor and I ate burgers and had first talked about the glaciers. I called the tour bus company from my room, reserved a single ticket for the next glacier tour. And the one after that.

"Every day," I said. "I want a seat on the glacier tour every day until the end of the season."

"Might make more sense for you to drive the bus yourself, don't you think?" the man said, then laughed.

It was two years later. Maybe three. The diner was full of locals. They sat in pairs and small groups, poker-faced. There was a girl about fifteen sitting with her parents in a booth near the back. She had red hair and freckles. Her hand rested on a well-worn paperback novel. She caressed it. Her mother was gray-headed, wore a denim jacket, deep ridges framing her face. Her father sat with his back to me, a cowboy hat atop his head. He was scolding the girl about the book, telling her to put it away while they ate.

I couldn't stop staring at the family. I felt the pressure of the girl's fingertips on that book. She was desperate to open it—I could feel her anticipation and desire to lose herself in a world unlike her own. As she gripped the book, she bottled her yearning, folded herself in. I could see her getting smaller.

What did the girl know—right then—about herself, about everything that mattered to her, that in ten years time might be lost? Warped. Her purity blackened and twisted until there was nothing inside her but irrepressible hunger and need, and for what, she might never be certain.

I stood and raised my camera. Zoomed in on her face. Before anyone could react, she showed me everything. Her fear, dread, hatred, hope, love: all of it.

And I took it. Snapped and captured it. I moved closer, my shutter firing like an automatic weapon.

Her mother yelled, but I didn't hear what. I kept snapping, moving closer, until I was just a foot from the girl's face. I eased the camera down; my naked eye met hers. By then she was lit from the inside. She understood. I'm sure she did. That remarkable first moment when someone has seen you, all the way to the core. It doesn't matter how long it lasts. It doesn't matter what happens next.

Her father's hands fell on my shoulders. Lifting, gripping, carrying. He pushed me out of the diner. I hit the concrete hard. Pain ricocheted through muscle and bone. I protected my camera as he hovered above me, his boot toe inches from my face.

"What are you, some kind of pervert? That's my daughter. Get the hell out of here!"

He spat on the ground, then went back inside, slamming the door behind him.

As I stood up, I felt the pain, the ache in my hip that would settle and stay. For years, as I drove that tour bus up and down the Icefields Parkway, thinking about algebraic geometry, scribbling in little notebooks in diners and coffee shops. An old, singular woman with a camera. For years, I would feel that ache in my hip and remember. The young girl sitting up so straight. Squaring her shoulders, clutching her paperback to her chest.

She beamed and she posed for me that day. And forever, I would hold the beauty inside.

# LEGS

I worked the midnight shift at the L'Eggs plant in Champaign. I stuffed pantyhose into plastic eggs all night because I needed the cash to cover tuition and rent and the occasional beer that, technically, I was too young to buy. The plant was next to the Kraft factory and the air stank of chemicals; it made me gag and sometimes crave grilled cheese sandwiches.

Eli was a townie from Rantoul. He'd worked at the plant for two years but he was new to the mid-shift. He smoked Kools and rode a Harley Fat Boy, called me College Girl. He was twenty-nine and lost, he told me, as he leaned his head back and blew smoke rings in the break room.

"Stay in school," he said. "Don't find yourself fingering hosiery at 4 a.m. when you're pushing thirty."

Laura Matfield sat across the room from us, her nose buried in an Anne Rice paperback again. Eli followed my eyes, tapped his cigarette pack.

"Interesting," he said.

"What?"

"The way you look at her. You're always looking but I ain't never seen you speak to her. Or her to you."

I didn't know what to say. I didn't trust easily.

Eli rolled his head to one side, bit the corner of his lip. "Makes me wonder if fingering *someone's* hosiery at 4 a.m. might be your idea of fun."

His usual scowl softened, and his smile was sincere, not mocking. So I took a chance, and nodded.

"All right," he said. "That's all right."

From that moment, we were friends.

Laura's fingers were thin. I studied the way she folded the ebony petites, so fast sometimes I could barely follow. She was a townie like Eli. At the end of each shift she stood at the curb outside the plant and waited for the same older woman in a rusted brown Camaro. Her mother, I guessed.

Laura was in her mid-twenties, older than me but not much. Her face was a little pocked from acne and her body was more plump than curvy. But there was something about the way she folded those ebony petites, as if she'd reached transcendence through the repetition. She was a master, tucking and folding, tucking and folding, her expression serene and confident. As I watched, I pictured her as different women, in different places, with different lives. I didn't have the best imagination but I'd watched a lot of TV. I could see her as Barbara Stanwyck reigning over a dust-bowl Western town, or as an explorer driving a Jeep in the Serengeti, stopping to photograph a lion's den from twenty feet. I wasn't sure where Laura went in her own mind but I was certain she wasn't in that plant in Champaign, Illinois. As she tucked and folded, tucked and folded, her feet were not bound to that concrete floor like the seventy-five other graveyard shifters. In the break room or standing at the curb, she was serious and sad. But on the line, working, she was different. She was someone.

I wanted to know her.

I rented a room in a crumbling house in Urbana. I had six housemates who weren't my friends. My landlady, Madge, was seventy-five and lived in the converted attic above my room. She sipped Scotch and listened to opera on vinyl. Every morning when I got home from the plant she asked if I'd stolen any queen-size nudes for her yet. No excuse satisfied her. Not even my last and most desperate plea, "I'm not a thief," which admittedly I only mumbled under my breath.

It was spring semester and I was only taking two classes. Even though it was too late for a full refund, I was on my way to the administration building to drop one of them. Intermediate French.

I didn't like to think about how many pairs of pantyhose I'd stuffed into little plastic eggs to pay for that class, but I couldn't take another minute of the humiliation. Professor Claire hated me. She said my French sounded like gruff guttural German. The truth was, I couldn't control my voice when she sat on top of her desk, staring at me. After last week, when she'd brushed her skirt against my hand as she handed back the exams, I was certain she was taunting me. Every class, she fed more intensely off my discomfort. I imagined her sipping red wine and telling the story to her husband, the one she updated nightly about the pathetic little lesbian who sat in the front row of French 102 and stared at Professor Claire's thighs as she crossed one leg over the other, before fumbling simple verb conjugations like an idiot. I imagined them laughing, toasting to the amusement. Then her husband would tell her to buy an even shorter skirt, stare at me even harder the next day.

Eli turned out to be a whiz at hosiery stuffing, just like Laura. I stood between them, Laura's agile hands folding briskly on my right, Eli's thick, tapered fingers scooping and tucking, scooping and tucking, on my left. I tried to stay focused on my work, my own quota. I trembled. It was only 1:15. The shift supervisor, Wayne, was watching me.

Wayne had a way of sensing who was about to crack. I'd seen him pull others off the line, scolding them for slowness and sloppy technique, giving warnings and probably docking pay. I tried to mimic Laura's movements, but my thumbs weren't flexible enough. I'd always gotten by before. Not the fastest, not the slowest either. Once Eli realized I had a thing for Laura, I was even more distracted. The way her hair fell gently across her face, the way she tossed it slightly to the side without thinking. I was mesmerized and soon, Wayne motioned for me to put the pantyhose down, follow him to the office.

Eli's eyes widened. Laura never looked up.

Wayne took me straight to his office. No side stops on the edge of the floor.

No first warning, I thought. He's just going to fire me. Then I'm dead. Forced to drop out of school. Unable to pay my rent.

Wayne laced his fingers across his breastbone, leaned back in his chair.

"You're a student at the university, right?" he asked.

My hands smelled of chemically-treated nylon. It was impossible to wash the stink off. Made me sick sometimes.

I nodded.

"You've been with us on mids for six months now, right?"

He knew the answers to his own questions, but I said, "Yes," obediently.

I stared at my hands and thought about how I'd never said a word to Laura and now it was too late. After I was fired, I'd never see her again.

"Your major, Miss Edwards? Do you have one?"

I looked up, realized I'd missed a question.

"Philosophy," I said. "It was mechanical engineering. But I recently changed to philosophy."

"That's quite a change," Wayne said. "Hadn't heard about the recent upturn in demand for philosophers."

He laughed until he made himself choke.

"I'm paying my own way now," I said. "Figured I should study what I wanted to study. It's my money."

Wayne regained himself.

"Sorry," he said. "Don't hear that one very often. You're an original, Miss Edwards. Just like I thought."

I wished Wayne would get it over with. Just fire me so I could get the hell out of there.

"I didn't mean any offense, Beth. You're smart. That's why you're here."

I startled at the sound of my first name. I'd never heard Wayne call anyone by their first name.

"I'll cut to the chase," he said. "You're not the best worker we have, you're not the fastest on the line, but neither was I. Truth is we've got plenty of fast stuffers. What we don't see everyday down here is smart. So here's the deal. We'd like to offer you a spot in our management training program. It would mean a bit of sacrifice at first. A switch to days, loss of shift-pay. But once you're through the program, you'll have a shot at supervisor. A decent raise. Your own office, like this—"

He waved his hands around, displaying the richness of his fortune. A steel desk that wobbled when he leaned on it, a squeaky chair, a window streaked with handprints, a view of the loading dock.

Wayne stood up, smoothed his shirt down, and said, "Think about it."

He shook my hand then pointed at the door.

I walked out, dizzy.

On our lunch break, Eli bought a frozen hamburger out of the vending machine and nuked it in the microwave. Said it tasted like mustard-flavored cardboard.

"PB&J," I said, holding up my sandwich. "Cheaper and better."

Laura was in the booth behind us. Ever since Eli started, she'd been moving closer at break time, edging over another booth every couple of days. Finally, she'd made it all the way to the booth next to us. Eli made faces at me, trying to draw my attention away from her. He bit into his burger with a cigarette still hanging from his lips.

"What did our old buddy Wayne have to say?"

"Nothing," I said.

"Nothing? He just took you into his office to stare at your handsome face?"

"I thought I was gonna get canned."

"Just a warning, then?"

"Yeah, a warning," I said, too self-conscious to tell him the truth.

Laura looked up from her novel, straight into my eyes. I'd just taken a huge bite of my sandwich; thick gobs of peanut butter clogged my throat. I began to cough and couldn't stop.

Eli pushed my soda toward me.

Laura stared.

I took a sip of my drink. Eli turned around.

"Would you like to join us?" he asked her.

I kicked him under the table.

Laura stared at Eli's cigarette, still dangling from his mouth, ashes about to fall.

He waved his arm behind him, toward me.

"Don't mind my friend here. She never spews peanut butter out of her nose more than once in a lunch period."

Laura didn't move.

Eli put his cigarette out, extended his hand across the back of the booth to her. "I'm Eli."

She shook his hand, kept looking at me. The peanut butter was gone but there was a growing pressure in my esophagus, as if something were trying to force its way up, or down.

"Wayne pulled you out," she said.

She talked so rarely, I was shocked at her voice; it was deeper than mine and rough, like sandy gravel. I wondered if she smoked, though I'd never seen her.

I nodded quickly.

"Everything okay?"

She was concerned? About me? I felt a rush, like a brisk wind through the center of my chest.

"Yeah, fine," I said. "It's fine."

"Good." She put her nose back in her book.

Eli finished his burger and winked at me.

At the end of our shift, my car wouldn't start. The damn engine sputtered and clanked, wouldn't engage. I'd just bought the rusted-out piece of crap from one of my roommates for a hundred bucks and as I'd suspected, he'd ripped me off. Laura stood next to Eli's bike. She looked like a schoolgirl, swaying against the breeze, one hand on her hip. Eli shaded his eyes from the sun. I got out of my car, opened the hood. I had no idea what to look for, didn't know anything about engines. I sure wished I could reach in, twiddle a wire, and turn my lousy lemon into a roaring racecar.

Eli slide-stepped across the parking lot in his heavy leather boots. "Need a ride?"

I slammed the hood.

He handed me his extra helmet and told me to get on the back of the bike, wrap my arms around his chest. Laura moved to her usual spot on the curb, waiting for the old lady in the Camaro. She kicked stones with her toe, not looking at us.

"Don't be shy," Eli said to me, pulling my arms tight around him. "Don't want you falling off."

I tried to make eye contact with Laura as we left but she didn't look up. I loosened my grip on Eli, wishing I had my own motorcycle. Wishing I wasn't such a child.

"I owe you one," I said, getting off the bike in front of my house. "Not that I'm good for a ride anywhere. I'll be back on the damn bus tomorrow."

I started to walk away, and Eli yelled after me. "Can I ask you something?"

I shrugged. "Sure."

"You ever actually been with a woman, kid?"

"What the hell kind of question is that?"

"I didn't think so."

"Fuck you!" I said.

"Hey, I didn't mean nothing. It's just, you're so goddamned wound up, it's pathetic. You gotta relax. Cool off a little."

I wanted to hit him but his eyes were too kind. He felt sorry for me, I could see that.

"You're off tonight, right?" he said.

"Yeah."

"I'm gonna pick you up around nine and take you out."

"In case you haven't been paying attention, I'm not interested in you."

"Don't be an idiot. I want to introduce you to some girls, fool. You have got to loosen up."

"I don't know—"

"Look. I know this place. Decent establishment. The girls love me." He slapped his fingers against his thigh and laughed. "Hell, they ought to. They get enough of my money."

"I have things to do tonight," I said.

"What? Like homework? Didn't you drop a class? Didn't you say you

44

barely had anything going on?"

I stared at the ground.

"Just be ready at nine," he said.

All through Early Modern Philosophy I thought about Eli and his girls, wondering what I was getting into. Eli and I were an odd pair to be friends, but he talked to me like a normal person. He didn't make me feel like a freak.

I checked out a gay and lesbian student meeting on campus once. The guys were only interested in each other and never said a word to me. The lesbians were all vegetarians and full of anger. They talked about "disenfranchisement" and the politics of body hair. I knew I was queer but I didn't find anyone like me at that meeting. I liked my steaks bloody. I shaved my legs because I liked the feel of my own smooth skin. I wore discount denim and leather from Goodwill. And when I looked in the mirror, I saw a slightly effeminate boy-face. I'd looked that way since I was nine and got my first short haircut. I imagined I would always be the ageless boy.

My philosophy professor was lecturing on Spinoza's ethics, the relativistic nature of good and evil. Spinoza said there was no absolute moral compass. It was all individual. Good for one, evil for another.

I watched the clock, tapped my pencil on the desk.

When Eli showed up at 9:15, I was waiting on the porch.

"How much money you got?" he said.

"I won't do it with a hooker, Eli."

He laughed. "It's just a titty bar, kid. That's all. But I can get you a private dance. I have a feeling that's all you need."

Riding on the back of the Harley, I held on to Eli. Kierkegaard's leap of faith. Infinity of self. Truth was, I didn't understand any of it. I thought changing my major would free me. That philosophy would explain the world. But I missed engineering. I missed doing a calculation and getting the right answer.

We drove about twenty minutes, way outside of town until there was nothing but corn on either side of us. The air enfolding us grew cooler and the farther we went, the blacker the night became. There is nothing darker than a vast Midwestern cornfield on a cool, moonless night.

The bar wasn't much bigger than the tiny break room at the plant. Thick smoke stung my eyes when we walked in. The music was loud, a funk rock blend with a heavy downbeat. In the parking lot, Eli said there was a particular girl he had in mind for me named Sheila.

"There's nothing wrong with you," he said. "You just need a little touch. That's all."

"Maybe it's not like that for me. Maybe I'm a lost cause."

He snickered. "We'll see."

We got a table near the stage. Eli ordered us beers and a shot of tequila for himself. The dancer was blonde and wore nothing but a G-string and high heels. She looked at me, squeezed her round breasts together, then winked. Eli nudged my arm, whispered, "Don't take your eyes off her."

She was dancing just for me. I was the only girl in the bar, other than the dancers. No one seemed to care. Eli put his hand on my back, touched my shoulder, and said, "Get out some ones. She likes you."

I pulled out my wallet and folded dollar bills into slits. The girl on the stage came toward me, bent over. I held up two dollars, uncertain what to do. She turned, slid her hip and the G-string toward my money. Eli nudged me. I slipped the dollar bills under the strap and she was gone, back up on the stage dancing, strolling to the other side of the bar where guys threw their hands in the air, clapping and cheering.

Eli put his arm around me. "Very nice."

We drank beers and watched the dancers and after about an hour I was out of singles and needed to pee. Eli came back from the bar carrying two more beers. "Buddy, I'm sorry. Sheila's not here tonight. Barkeep just told me."

"It's okay," I said.

The women's restroom was near the back door. Two stalls and not much room to move. From inside, I heard the burst of music as the door opened. I saw high heels. Through the door slit, legs. I wedged myself out of my stall. Leaning against the wall, she winked at me, the same way she had from the stage.

"First time here?"

"Yeah." I straightened out my shirt. She was tall, and her thighs were shaded perfect pantyhose taupe.

"Want a dance?" she asked.

Her nipples were at my eye level. I managed to say, "Yeah, sure. Can I wash my hands?"

She stepped aside, and I went to the sink. Tried my best not to look at her through the mirror as I soaped my hands, twice.

We walked back into the bar together. I stopped at the table, and said,

"Private dance," to Eli.

He grinned and gave me a ridiculous salute. I followed the dancer into a back room with a shredded old couch and a lava lamp. I was glad it was dark.

She explained the rules and asked for the twenty-five bucks up front. I gave it to her and promised not to touch, to keep my hands by my sides as she instructed. I sat on the couch. She danced a little standing up in front of me, watching me, touching her breasts, her stomach, then closing her eyes and grabbing her crotch. There was an odd split in my mind. Turned on. Ashamed.

But when she moved toward me, climbed on top of me, and slid her body flush against mine, I didn't care about the shame. The sensation overwhelmed. The brush of her skin against my clothes, exchanging pressure with rhythm, back and forth, up and down. I tried to picture one of those hairy-legged lesbians from the meeting in my position and I sure couldn't. But I was there, right there with the dancer, and she kept looking at me. She moved and writhed and I stared into those soft brown eyes and there was nothing shameful about it. She eased me farther back against the couch, pressing harder and faster, harder and faster. Her hips, belly, breasts grinding into me. It came on instantly, like an explosion. I lurched forward, cried out. My heart pounded harder than it ever had.

The dancer smiled.

I held my hands up, and said, "I didn't touch."

She cupped my face in her hands, and said, "I know, baby. I know."

She kept going, slower. Pressing firm against me. Not letting up.

Eli was right. The dance was all I needed.

When she was done, I opened my wallet and gave her two more twenties. She laughed, leaned down and kissed me. I smiled but didn't touch her. I watched her walk away, her legs growing longer and more lovely with every step she took.

On the way home, Eli stopped at a Waffle House. We drank coffee and he smoked. He asked about my family, about why a College Girl like me worked midnights in a factory to pay my own tuition. So I told him. I told him about my father who died when I was ten, about my clinically depressed mother who couldn't get over it. Until she found Jesus and a born-again pharmaceutical executive named Phil who had three grown daughters of his own and tried to force me to grow my hair long and wear pink skirts like they all did. About how my mom and Phil lived comfortably in a high-rise condominium overlooking Lake Michigan. And when I'd told them six months ago that I was gay, they stopped sending me money, stopped taking my calls. Phil said I was on my own unless I repented for my sins and accepted Jesus Christ as my personal savior. And my mother didn't argue.

"Fuck," Eli said, stubbing his cigarette out. "Fuck, man, I'm sorry."

I shrugged. "Give me one of those Kools."

He lit a cigarette for me and I tried to inhale. Gagged instead. I laughed.

He patted me on the back, and said, "You're a good kid."

I inhaled again, and smoke filled my lungs. "Tonight I accepted Rose Anna as my personal savior."

"Was that her name? She's new. She had the hots for you."

Eli was full of shit but I wasn't going to argue with him.

"You feel better, huh? You look cool as a cucumber now, my friend. Ready to take on the world."

"You're nuts," I said. "But I'd do it again."

"So much for lost causes."

Eli paid for our coffees and we got back on the bike and drove into the darkness of corn.

A tow truck retrieved my car from the L'Eggs parking lot and the mechanic declared it needed a thousand dollars worth of work to make it drivable. I paid the junk yard twenty bucks to haul it away, bought a monthly pass for the bus, and told the roommate who'd sold the car to me that he was an asshole.

A few days later I found myself sitting on a bench across from the language building. I didn't plan on being there at that particular time. Maybe it was just a subconscious habit, being in that spot just before Professor Claire's Intermediate French class.

I saw her before she saw me. She was coming down Mathews Avenue. I focused on her short skirt, her long legs. As she got closer, I looked up and met her eyes. I didn't look away. Her mouth opened slightly, as if she were about to speak. She kept walking, passed me, then turned back. I held my stare and when she finally disappeared into the Foreign Language Building, I leaned back on the bench, and laughed.

Laura missed work for a few nights in a row and I began to worry. I wondered if she was sick or if she'd quit or if they'd asked her to move to the day shift and she'd said yes. On the fourth night of her absence, I went to ask Wayne if she was all right. It was the end of my shift and the day crew was clocking in. Wayne stood outside his office, talking with a guy I'd never seen. A young black man in a suit and tie who held a clipboard and asked Wayne questions. When I walked up, Wayne looked happy to see me. I asked about Laura and he said her mother had passed away. She was out for the funeral.

"Oh," I said. "I'm sorry to hear that."

Wayne turned to the man in the suit. "Beth, I'd like you to meet someone. This is Stephen Johnston from corporate. He works in Quality Control."

The man held out his hand, and I shook it.

"What did you say your degree was in, Mr. Johnston?" Wayne asked.

"Industrial and Systems Engineering. I just graduated last year."

Wayne nodded, appearing proud of himself, as if he were the one with the degree and the clipboard.

"You have to wear a suit everyday?" I asked the man.

He laughed. "Nah. Not every day."

"Given any thought to our offer, Miss Edwards?" Wayne said.

"I'm still in school. You think I could do the management program and still take classes? I'm thinking of switching majors again."

"We can talk about it," Wayne said. "You let me know if you're serious. It's a good company. Wouldn't you agree, Johnston?"

Johnston didn't look up from his clipboard. He was lost in his columns of numbers and calculations. I knew what industrial engineers did. It wasn't like building a bridge or designing a computer, but it was something. Something I was pretty sure I could do better than stuffing hose into plastic eggs or understanding philosophy.

When Laura finally showed up back at work she sat on the other side of the break room again, reading a new novel. Science fiction this time.

"Go talk to her," Eli said. "You know you want to."

I shook my head, No. She was shy and she'd just lost her mother and it didn't matter how many lap dances I'd had. I would still make an ass of myself if I walked over to her table.

Eli blew smoke in my face. "Idiot," he said.

I gripped the booth bench, dug my nails into the particle board.

For the rest of the shift, I cursed myself under my breath. Locke said all knowledge comes through experience. So I'd had a private dance. So I'd conquered my fear of Professor Claire. I still didn't know how to talk to a girl I liked, someone I wanted to get to know. I couldn't pretend she was a half-naked dancer. The money in my pocket wasn't going to make her smile at me.

I was still a blank slate when it came to love.

I rushed out of the plant before Eli could offer me a ride home on his bike. I felt like a failure and I didn't want him to be nice to me. I started off toward the bus stop when I heard the heavy roar of the Camaro behind me. It pulled up beside me, stopped. All the windows were down.

"My stupid mother loved this car," Laura said. She started to cry.

I stood there, paralyzed on the sidewalk for a minute. Then I stepped closer, leaned against the passenger's side door.

"I'm so sorry about your mom," I said.

"She was only 58. Heart attack. Just like that. Your heart's beating, then it's not."

She wiped tears away. "I wasn't very fast on the line today," she said. "Couldn't concentrate."

I nodded. My throat went dry. Laura Matfield and I were having a conversation.

Her eyes were grayish-blue, like denim. I'd never been close enough to tell before.

"Can I give you a ride somewhere?" she said. "I'm not used to being in this car alone yet."

My breath was shallow but I managed to say, "Sure. Thanks."

After I got in, she just sat there, looking hollow and lost.

"It's all different now," she said. "You just never know when something is going to happen that changes your whole life."

I gripped the car seat beneath me and took a deep breath. "I know."

She brushed her hair away from her face.

From an unfathomable depth, my courage rose up, and I heard myself say: "My name's Beth. I don't think we've ever formally met, and I've wanted to change that for quite awhile."

She looked into my eyes, and her tension slipped away. There she was, as I'd seen her on the L'Eggs plant floor so many times. Peaceful. Confident. Strong.

"It's nice to meet you, finally. I'm Laura."

She put the car in gear.

# SITTING FOR WANDA

"You sure you can handle this?"

I sat cross-legged on a patchwork quilt at the center of my sister Wanda's waterbed, feeling seasick. I nodded, saying "Yeah, of course. It's cool."

Wanda buzzed around the room, tossing T-shirts into her blue suitcase, talking about her next "amazing opportunity." It was 1979 and my sister Wanda was a groupie for rock 'n roll bands touring up and down the eastern seaboard. She'd just told me–in graphic detail–what that meant, and I sort of wished she hadn't.

She'd made it all the way to New Jersey once, but usually it was just Florida, Georgia, maybe South Carolina. Long before she told me the details, I knew what she did on her "amazing opportunity" trips. She didn't have any money and she'd somehow seen every band that ever played a concert within 500 miles. Dozens of backstage passes lined a bulletin board in her kitchen.

Wanda wanted me to watch her cats while she was gone, and that was fine. Her house was just a few blocks from ours and I didn't mind. But Wanda's trips were getting longer, and she was growing more frenetic before each one. I was starting to worry about her.

Up and down I bobbed as the waterbed rocked. Wanda yanked a pink and grey parka out of the hamper, sniffed it.

"You have to leave tonight?" I asked.

"Bus rolls at midnight, Kiddio."

She stuffed red frilly panties in the suitcase. "I showed you what to do about the doggie door, right? Gotta keep the chair propped in front of it, or God knows what will wander in."

"Yeah. Got it."

"What am I forgetting?"

She collapsed next to me, letting her long black hair fall into my lap.

Upside down her lip-glossed mouth looked slippery, as if it might slide right off her face if she wasn't careful.

"Ellie? What am I forgetting?"

"Don't worry. I can handle the cats." Just as well, if not better. At fifteen, I was more trustworthy than her or any of her stoner friends. She was twenty-one and still working at Burger King.

"The plants! Fuck! The fucking plants!" Wanda jumped off the bed and bounded down the hall to retrieve her crops. After flailing around for at least ten minutes, she put them in the bathtub.

"Keep the door closed and water them every day. Don't let the cats near them!"

"It'll be fine," I said. "Don't worry."

Wanda sunk her black-painted fingernails into my back as she pulled me in for a hug. "My God, El, don't let Mom and Dad in that fucking bathroom!"

"They won't come over here."

"I know, I know. Shit! I can't believe I'm laying this trip on you. It's just a really important trip for me. This new band—they're really breaking out. They could be huge soon. Stars!"

"It's fine. I got it, Sis."

I'd never smoked weed before. If I ever wanted to, all I had to do was ask, Wanda told me a million times. Stoners should never be stingy with their stash, she'd say. Bad karma.

I walked from Wanda's place to ours. The sun was setting purple-magenta over the short stucco houses. The neighborhood was post-war tract style, with waist-high chain-link fences defining the yards and pink flamingos dotting the lawns. The smell of saffron rice and pork roast wafted out of our neighbor's kitchen window.

Inside, my mother was taking TV dinners out of the oven and Dad was asleep in his ratty old recliner, a copy of *Field and Stream* on his chest.

"Salisbury steak," Mom said as I slipped past her to my small room. "Ready in five."

We ate on TV trays and watched "Happy Days" and my dad laughed whenever Potsie did something stupid. "That kid cracks me up," he'd say.

After dinner, my father raised an eyebrow. "Homework?"

"Finished it."

"All of it?" He stared at the TV, then smiled in sync with the canned sitcom laugh track.

"Would I lie?" I said, snapping a TV tray shut in front of him.

"Don't get fresh with your father," Mom said, sticking her head in from the kitchen. "He saw Wanda today at the 7-Eleven so he's not in the mood."

The "Happy Days" glow faded. "She's got no sense at all," Dad said. "Tell me you won't turn out that way, baby."

He reached for my hand. "I don't know what I did wrong with that girl. I just don't—"

I sat down on the arm of the recliner, wrapped my arms around his heavy shoulders. I kissed his forehead. "I'm nothing like Wanda, Dad."

He squeezed my hand. "I know. I just worry. It's a Dad thing."

Fonzie slid onto the screen and Potsie scurried behind Richie Cunningham and squealed. My father's arms flew up, knocking me off the side of his chair.

I finished my algebra homework in the ten minutes between the bell ending the official school day and the beginning of symphonic band practice. I was, according to my father, "too smart for my own good." It wasn't something I tried to accomplish or anything. I just made A's without trying very hard. Mom said I was their reward for not killing Wanda when she was a teenager. I just hoped my good grades would land me a full scholarship to a college far, far away. I didn't hate my parents. I was just tired of everything being so shabby, so run-down.

My middle school math teacher, Mr. Gonzalez, never stopped talking about how math and science were the key to landing a good-paying job. "You want a nice car? Do your math homework! You want a swimming pool in your backyard? Study physics or chemistry. Every successful person I know did well in math or science, or both. I'm not bullshitting you kids. I'm dead serious." I don't know if anyone else listened to Mr. Gonzalez's shit like I did. I was rapt, finally grateful for all the nerdy things that came so naturally, like acing algebra without much effort. Music, on the other hand, wasn't a gift for me. I practiced hard and didn't entirely suck, but I clearly lacked natural talent.

After slipping my math book into my bag, I began assembling my clarinet. From my position at second chair I had a great view of Alan Ramone, third chair trombone. I liked to watch him warm up before practice. He brushed his shoulder length wheat-colored hair back from his face and moistened his lips before touching them to his mouthpiece, leaving them poised in position to pucker and play. Alan was a quiet guy. Not popular, but not a loser either. He was aloof and disinterested in the band boys' shenanigans. Never saw him teasing anyone or gossiping. All of that won him cool points with me.

Alan caught me watching him. I flipped through my sheet music, aiming for nonchalant.

Looking back, I thought he might have winked at me. My knee jerked in response, bumping my black metal music stand into Maggie Mitchell's back.

Maggie, first chair flute and supreme snob, spun around and shot me a look.

"Sorry," I said, righting my stand.

I caught Alan's eye again and smiled. He held my gaze longer than usual. A new development, and I had to admit, I liked it.

Mr. Phelps stepped to the podium and raised his baton. "Kentucky 1800," an old-style favorite with the trumpet jerks, sounded better than usual that day.

I was putting my reed into its small plastic case when Maggie nudged me. "Here he comes," she said. "Hope you know what you're doing."

I blew warm air into my clarinet mouthpiece to dry it off, trying not to look at Alan as he approached.

"Hey," he said.

I echoed a soft "hey" in reply.

"Heading home now?" He asked.

"Yeah."

"I could walk you. If you want?"

Two blocks from school, he took my hand in his. My palm was sweaty and his was dry and warm. Our fingers interlocked. He was taller than I'd realized, probably six inches taller than me or more. I'd never been this close to him before and I didn't know what to do. I decided to take him to Wanda's. Being alone with him at her house seemed less horrifying than introducing him to my dad, who was temporarily "between jobs" and always seemed to be watching "Gilligan's Island" when I got home from school.

"I'm taking care of my sister Wanda's cats while she's out of town," I said. "It's only three more blocks."

"Great," he said, squeezing my knuckles with his.

As I struggled with the key in the front door, Alan stood patiently on the cement steps behind me.

"Dammit," I said, kicking the door.

"Want me to try?"

I stepped aside. He held the knob steady and jiggled the key with his thumb, then turned the knob. It opened right up. He stepped back and let me go in first. I liked that he didn't gloat or say anything stupid. He just pushed the door open and smiled.

Wanda had left the radio on for the cats, Yoko and Stevie. The opening bars of "Stairway to Heaven" played at a volume more appropriate for Muzak than Led Zeppelin. When I came around the corner, I gasped.

Sitting on the kitchen table, licking his balls, was a large orange tomcat that did not belong to Wanda.

"What?" Alan said, stepping in behind me.

"Shit. The doggie door—" I said.

Alan walked up and started to stroke the tomcat on the top of his head. The cat meowed and rolled over, stretching out for a belly rub.

"He doesn't belong here," I said. "Wanda needs to board up that damn door. That big tom pushed his way past the chair we'd propped in front."

I went over to the cat bowls and picked them up. "He ate all the food, too."

Alan picked up the matted orange tabby and walked to the front door. I heard the door open, then slam shut.

"All gone," he said.

"You want a Coke?"

Alan put his hand on my shoulder. When I turned around, he was right there. I didn't move. His hand slid to my elbow. His lips were full and moist. Trombone lips. I stepped closer and he put his arms around my waist. We kissed. And kissed and kissed and kissed some more. He held his jaw tight, his mouth forming a perfect rigid oval. No tongue, no probing or groping. Just slow, steady open-mouth kissing. I let my hand move slowly down his back. I took a half-step and slid my leg between his.

He stopped, took a step back, straightening himself out. "Where's the bathroom?" he said.

The bathroom. Shit. The pot plants were all over the place. What would he think? Would he freak out? Would he want to harvest himself a joint?

"Toilet's broken," I said.

He turned around and yanked at his shirt, ran his hand through his thick hair. "You're kidding—" he said. "I really have to go."

"Sorry."

His face was red and he looked sick. "I've gotta go—"

As the front door slammed behind him, the big orange tomcat who didn't belong jumped back through the doggie door, trotted through the living room, and hopped up on the kitchen table.

The next day I was late to band practice because Marsha Engles kept asking me stupid questions about our American History homework while I was shoving my books into my locker. I hated walking in late. It drew too much attention and interfered with my ability to stay invisible to the dorky trumpet-playing boys who were always looking for a target.

After an hour of the band butchering Mr. Phelps' latest obsession, "September" by Earth, Wind, and Fire, he tossed his plastic baton down and stormed off the podium. Everyone looked around the room, wondering if practice was over or whether Mr. Phelps was going to come charging back, pumping his fists in 3/4 time for another thirty minutes.

I looked over at the trombones. Alan's horn was propped against his knee and Pete Biggs, second chair trumpet, was standing next to him, whispering in his ear. Alan stared straight ahead, emotionless. The trumpet gang in front of him started nudging each other, giggling. Pete pointed at me and the trumpet boys laughed in synchrony, more precisely timed than their playing ever was. I strained to hear what Pete and his horn-ball brigade were saying. I couldn't make it out but I was pretty sure I knew. Too many kids at my school had older siblings who knew Wanda. I started breaking down my clarinet, gathering up my books.

"Is it true?" Jenny Ferguson, the lone French horn, snuck up behind me.

"Is what true?"

"That your sister's a groupie like Pete said?"

I looked back toward the brass section. Pete blew me a kiss and laughed, the rest of the trumpeters each following suit. Six blown kisses and a devious cackling floating across the practice hall. Everyone stared at me.

"He said his brother was a roadie for Tom Petty last year and your sister—"

I grabbed Jenny by the arm, and said, "Shut up, already."

She started to speak and I gathered as much venom in my stare as I could manage. Holding onto Jenny's arm, I turned and saw Alan towering over Pete. He laid his hand on Pete's shoulder and nodded toward the door. I'd never seen Pete so pale.

Jenny pulled away from me. I grabbed my case and book bag and bolted, running as fast as I could to Wanda's house.

As soon as I unlocked the front door I knew something wasn't right. The place usually smelled a little stale, but not this bad—rancid high-concentrate urine—so strong it made my eyes water.

From the kitchen, I could see the bathroom door standing wide open. I ran to the scene of the crime.

"Oh. My. God." I said, pulling the shower curtain back.

One of the marijuana plants was nearly half gone, leaves shredded and gnawed; the other was dripping wet. Judging from the smell and several tufts of dander around the rim of the tub, the perpetrator appeared to be feline in origin. I tried to picture Wanda's face.

Very bad karma. *Very bad*, I could hear her say.

"Hello?" The bathroom door moved behind me, and I jumped.

"Jesus!" I yelled, turning to find Alan standing in the doorway.

"I knocked and the front door slid right open," he said, holding his nose. "What is that?"

"Cat piss," I said, trying to slip the shower curtain shut. It was too late.

Alan peeked around me, seeing the mutilated plants. "Oh, man. Bummer—"

"My sister's gonna kill me. I guess I didn't close the bathroom door tight last night. Had to be that damn tomcat."

"The toilet in here isn't really broken, is it?"

"No," I said.

He laughed a little, then one corner of his mouth folded into a half-frown. "You could have told me. I'm not a narc. And I really did have to pee—I ended up whizzing on your neighbor's tree."

"Sorry," I said, with a shrug.

Alan bent down to examine the plants. "Nice couple—male and female—great for a steady crop. That little fucker really munched on the mother ship, though."

I raised an eyebrow. "Male and female? You can tell them apart?"

Alan touched the half-eaten plant. "Females have these little hairs." He moved to the other plant. "And males have flowers."

"Flowers?"

"Yeah, look."

I leaned down next to him.

"They have sex?" I said.

He laughed. "Sort of. They have pollination."

"Oh, right," I said, slipping my hand into my jeans pocket. "God, I can't stand that smell. I'm gonna get some cleaning stuff from the kitchen."

I came back with Mr. Clean, rags, and a mop. Alan was in the tub, gathering up the loose-leaf pieces and stacking them in a neat pile in the palm of his hand.

"Hand me a towel," he said.

He laid the towel out on the counter and started lining up broken leaves, slowly patting them dry.

"You don't have to do that," I said. "I can clean it up."

"This is prize weed, Ellie. I'm honored to help."

"Who the hell *are* you?"

"My big brother's a Dead Head. I've been bagging weed since I was ten." He had the cutest set of dimples when he smiled.

"About band today—" I said, looking down at the tile floor.

"Pete Biggs is an ass and he can't play the trumpet worth shit."

No argument there.


Alan insisted we hand dry every leaf, keeping as much of the living plants intact as possible. He moved the plants over to the bathroom counter and I got out Wanda's old hair dryer. He held the leaves firm while I blew them dry, then he patted them down again with the towel. I was ready to call it quits after the urine smell started to fade, but Alan turned out to be a perfectionist. I sat on the toilet seat lid, watching him harvest leaves and seeds into a ziplock bag, trimming and pruning the damaged plant.

"That's the best I can do," he said, finally stopping.

"Amazing."

"I hope your sister is okay with it. When's she coming back?"

"Tomorrow, I think."

He nodded.

The bathroom felt cramped when he moved closer to me. I wasn't sure what to say. I wanted him to kiss me again, or make some indication that he wanted to, but he just stood there staring at the weed.

"You wanna try some?" I asked. "It might taste like cat piss."

He bit his lip. "Most of the good stuff smells like shit. Literally. Like manure. Same difference."

He took the ziplock bag to the kitchen table. His hands flew into a fast-forward flurry of activity. I sat on the lumpy brown couch in the living room and flipped on the TV. Fred and Wilma were at the drive-in movies eating a rack of brontosaurus ribs.

"Maybe we should dry a batch really good overnight and save it for when your sister gets back," Alan said.

"Whatever."

Alan stared at the table like it was a crystal ball foretelling his future.

"I should go." He stood up.

I turned off the TV. He was already at the front door. "Why are you rushing off?"

He shrugged.

I stepped towards him and put my hand on his arm. He leaned down and kissed me hard, his tongue plunging into my mouth like a dam bursting. He pushed me back against the wall and I wrapped my arms around his waist. Pressure was building against my thigh. He was hard already. I hadn't even thought he was going to kiss me, and suddenly he was pushing his hands up under my shirt, squeezing my breasts through the thick cotton of my padded A cups.

I pushed him away slightly, because I thought that's what I was supposed to do. He kept kissing me, kept pressing against me. I grabbed his hand and pulled him towards the couch. I fell back against the tattered upholstery and he dropped on top of me, pushing me into a reclining position.

I wished I had a slow-motion button. I wished he would take as much time with me as he took drying those marijuana leaves. Rolling the seeds between his fingers, patting the branches dry with the clean white towel. He wasn't like that with me. He clumsily unzipped his fly and pulled it out while I pulled down my jeans. Two swift pumps and he was done. Then he made some lame excuse about homework and left. I thought the first time would be something to remember. I was sure wrong about that.

I cleaned up the mess strewn all over the kitchen table, put food down for the cats, and walked home, listening to a chorus of crickets calling out in the night. I tried not to think about Alan, or Wanda's weed, or stupid trumpet-playing dweebs.

The thing I kept thinking about, though, was that damned orange tomcat licking his balls on the kitchen table and smiling a stupid stoner smile like one of Wanda's ex-boyfriends.

I skipped school the next day and hid out at Wanda's house. I wasn't sure I wanted to return to symphonic band. I was sick of playing the clarinet anyway. It squealed when I hit a sour note.

I lay on Wanda's couch watching soap operas all afternoon. Alan's musty odor lingered on the sofa cushions. I wasn't sure if I liked it or if it was making me sick, but every time I got up and came back to the sofa I sniffed the cushions again to see if it was still there.

I must have fallen asleep because I didn't hear Wanda until the scream.

Slasher horror movie scream. I sat straight up, adrenaline flooding me wide awake.

Her suitcase sat against the wall. When I got to the bathroom, she was sitting on the toilet seat with her head in her hands.

"We did the best we could," I said.

She looked up at me, and I could tell she'd been crying for days, not minutes. Her face was splotchy with dried mascara.

"We?"

I tried to explain quickly, hitting the cat piss angle hard. Cursing the doggie door, emphasizing that it wasn't my fault—there was no keeping that damned tomcat out—he just kept coming back, again and again. The stench still lingered in the air. Then I moved to Alan, focusing on the clean-up operation. Given her rough appearance, I wasn't sure she could handle the part about me losing my virginity on her sofa just yet.

I made her some hot tea with honey and we ate graham crackers at the kitchen table.

"I'm glad you're back," I said.

"Me too." She looked older and puffier, like she'd gained five years in three days.

I didn't know what to say to her. How to fill that silence that always sat so heavy between us.

Wanda sat in the straight wooden chair, pouring honey onto her graham cracker and staring out the window. I laid my head on her shoulder.

"I'm gonna take a shower," she said. "Help me move the plants?"

As we set the potted plants under the window in her bedroom, Wanda finally exhaled, and said, "I sure wish that damn cat had just eaten the male plant. Males are so easy to replace. But it's gonna take a lot to get Momma Jane going again."

She kissed the top of my head, a touch of affection that caught me off-guard.

I started to tell her more about Alan. What happened, how disappointing it was.

Before I could, she said, "That kid you brought over here—he knows too much about weed to be a good boyfriend. You know that, right?"

This didn't sound anything like my sister. I tried not to imagine what could have happened while she was gone. I knew it was bad, and I couldn't face it. Not yet.

Instead, I just squeezed her hand, leaned forward, and said, "Yeah, I know."

# FLARES

There are some connections that defy all explanation, my mother said. I was sixteen and she was thirty-eight, about to die. We sat at the kitchen table and she held my hands. There are people who will blaze into your life and shine like flares on the highway, she told me. You'll know it when it happens. There will be no question whether it's love or whether it's real or whether it will last. The people who decimate your heart do it in a single glance. A gesture. A word. It will stay with you forever. When you're eighty-nine and a respirator is working your lungs to breathe, or you're forty-five and cancer has ravished your body, you will dream of that moment and know that you lived.

My mother and I looked at photo albums, back to front, working from present to past. She stopped on the second page of the first book to caress the only picture of my father I'd ever seen. He was holding six-month-old me in his arms and smiling as if there were a lifetime of love in his heart.

"He wasn't a bad man," my mother said. "He just had promises to keep. It's good to love a man who keeps his promises."

But his promises were not to us. They were to his wife and three other children and my mother's failing health had nothing to do with that, she told me. The muscle her doctors called her heart was defective, it always had been. It would give out before she rose to the top of the transplant list. *Be ready*, she said.

*Be prepared.*

Now I'm in a dusty bar decorated with surf boards and hula skirts. There's a view of the Pacific Ocean just outside the window but I'm not watching the waves, or the sunset, or the California palms. I'm watching my mother's hands hold a whiskey glass in front of me. I see the hands shake. I feel the warmth of her smile as she stands at our old kitchen counter chopping celery, sliding it into the crock pot with those long slender fingers, the same fingers that struggle to grip my Jim Beam.

Three stools down, a guy with a porn star mustache sticks his thumb into his drink, then sucks it. On the other side, a man with a weathered brow loosens his tie and slips off his wedding band, cranes his neck to see if anyone noticed. The bartender is a woman my age, heavy-set and gruff. She pours me another whiskey. Amber is such a soothing color. Molten lava in a glass.

I'm glad Daniel kept the house in Atlanta, glad for the five-hour plane ride between us. Glad for a quick divorce, glad for a new job in a new city where the sun shines more than 260 days a year. *Can that be right?*

The guy with the loosened tie approaches, says "Hi." His eyes are flat and cold. I imagine him a lawyer, losing a big case, needing to forget. Doesn't want to fight with the wife so he's here, hoping the gray at his temples and the body he still pushes hard at the gym will score him someone uninhibited and accommodating.

I nod at the bartender, open the Lyft app on my phone.

"Let me drive you," the man says.

The bartender wipes down the countertop, points toward the door. "Drivers case this joint all the time. One's already here, love."

The man puts his hand on my arm. "Go home," I say, and pull away.

The streetlight above the car glows a different sort of amber. Electric halo, shining like Saturn's rings.

My mother's thirty-two and I'm ten and she's telling me I shouldn't be so particular about my friends. *People will surprise you,* she whispers, as I rest my head against the car window. *You might even surprise yourself. If you try.*

On Saturday, the drapes are closed because the goddamned California sun is blinding as a comet. I've watched the same infomercial three times and I'm convinced that there really *is* unlimited wealth potential in real estate and I *would* begin today, if I had the energy to move my legs a single inch.

There's a knock at my door. I turn up the volume on the TV and hope whoever it is will go the hell away. The knock persists. I think about getting up but don't. There's a large yellow dog barking on the TV as a young girl runs through a suburban backyard, tugging clothes off the line.

The knock moves to the window and I wonder if I should be scared. I don't know anyone in San Diego. I moved into this apartment three weeks ago. I don't know anyone in California. Or the entire West Coast.

It's an ad for laundry detergent. Dirt, grass stains, doggie foot prints.

The knock moves back to the door. One quick tap, a last-ditch effort. I peek out. A woman stands there, looking at her sneakers. Short brown hair, Mickey Mouse sweatshirt, faded jeans. The sun behind her hits my retinas and stings. I recoil and close the drapes. My reflection in the mirror frightens me.

*Answer the door*, my mother says. Her voice is strong. Insistent. *I didn't teach you to be this rude.*

I'm alone, Mother. I don't know this woman.

There's no more knocking, so I put my hand on the door and count to ten, hoping she'll be gone by the time I open it. She's not.

She seems shocked at my appearance but doesn't look away. "Sorry to bother you," she says. "I'm Lindsay, your next-door neighbor."

She bends down to a bouquet of flowers on the ground. I think maybe it's a welcome gift, and wonder: Do people in Southern California do this sort of thing? Is this boyish woman I've never met really giving me flowers? For no reason other than I'm here, living next door to her?

"You weren't home yesterday and they left these with me," she says. "I tried last night, too, but—"

A delivery. Of course. Once I see the mixture of red roses and white orchids, I don't have to look at the card.

"My ex-husband," I say. "Trying to save his soul."

Lindsay shoves her hands in her pockets. "Nice to meet you," she says, walking away.

"You want some coffee?" The words come out before I can stop them. I haven't been friendly to anyone, not even the people I call friends, in over a year. Not since I caught Daniel going down on his receptionist in the middle of our king-size bed on top of the quilt we bought at a Dutch market on our second wedding anniversary. It was hand-stitched, beautiful. I loved that fucking quilt.

Lindsay stops halfway between her door and mine. "Sure. I'd love some coffee," she says.

I look back in my apartment. "I don't think I have any, actually—"

She smiles, almost blushing. Her eyes are warm and brown and full of something I haven't seen in a long time. Tenderness, perhaps. Innocence. She runs her fingers through her wavy hair, motions for me to follow her.

"Wait—I can't go out like this," I say. "I look like hell."

"Just to the corner. Jack-in-the-Box. Cheap and hot. My favorite."

I feel like a homeless person, stinking of the previous night's alcohol, wearing sweatpants crusted with Stouffer's French Bread pizza from three days ago and sneakers with holes bigger than my toes. Lindsay buys our coffees because I walked off with no money. I am a charity case, a bum.

I sit in a booth and try to mat my hair down against my head. She brings the coffee on a tray with cream and sugar, little pink packets of Sweet 'N Low, a dozen swizzle sticks, and napkins.

"Need anything else?" she asks.

I laugh.

She stirs her own coffee, wipes wet spots off the table. "What's funny?" she says.

"Nothing. I'm just losing my mind."

She leans back. "I don't know your name," she says. "If you're going to lose your mind in front of me, I should probably know your name."

"Jessica. No, not really. Jess. My name is Jess and despite appearances, I am employed. I own clean clothes. And on alternate Tuesdays, I'm reasonably sane."

Lindsay smiles again. "Tuesdays. I'll remember that."

"Alternate Tuesdays. Not every one."

Lindsay turns out to be a software engineer at a biotech in Mission Valley. Recently split with her partner, Rachel. They'd been together ten years.

"Daniel and I only lasted three," I say.

She listens as I tell my predictable story, nodding in the appropriate places, not interrupting or injecting opinions. She's a good listener. The best I've met in years.

I don't mention the quilt, or the fact that I stuffed it into a metal trash can, placed it in the center of our pristinely landscaped backyard, and burned it to ashes the night I kicked Daniel out of our home. It's the best part of the story but there's only so much crazy I can share on first meeting.

We take our time, sipping our coffee. Nearly an hour goes by. When we get back to the apartments, she pulls her wallet out of her back pocket and hands me a business card.

"I'm right next door," she says. "And my work number's on the card. If you need anything—"

She thinks I'm kidding about losing my mind, I suppose. About everything not covered on alternate Tuesdays.

I tuck the card in my pocket, and say, "Thanks." Never intending to call.

Inside, I don't look at Daniel's flowers. I don't read his card. I don't give my mother enough time to whisper in my ear. I go straight to the cabinet, pull out a bottle full of amber reflections. I pour and I drink and I pour and I drink and I pour.

It will not go away. It is September 17th. All day it has been September 17th.

Four years ago today, I married him. Four years ago today, I believed in love.

My mother would have forgiven Daniel for everything. Had she been me—or I been her—she would have taken all his weaknesses and wrapped her love around them. She wouldn't have held a grudge and she wouldn't have abandoned the marriage. She would have made the bastard soup and hot tea and told him it would all be just fine.

I tell this to Lindsay as we sit in a bar in Hillcrest, sipping margaritas and watching women slow dance together. I don't know why I let her bring me here, but after three drinks, I don't care. There are no men at the bar with loosened ties or tan lines around their ring fingers.

I'm wearing jeans and a loose silk blouse I bought at Macy's in New York City (the only time I'd ever been) and I've never had more sideways glances in a single night, anywhere. It's not a bad feeling, all these women watching me. I'm surprised to find that I like it when Lindsay leans in, close enough to smell her citrus perfume (or is that men's cologne?).

"Mothers don't always know best," she says, sliding her hand across the table, stopping just short of mine. She's brazen when tipsy. She's a risk taker and I appreciate that.

I finish my margarita.

"Another?" she says.

"Sure."

We get up and dance to a few old 80s tunes. Bouncy, silly songs, where the dancing is more communal than intimate. I like the way the lights on the floor sparkle and reflect a prism on the wall.

How did I get here? How many days fell between Daniel's flowers and Jack-in-the-Box coffee and now? Did Lindsay call me, or did I call her? I wonder if I could go to bed with her.

So many women spiral around us. Tall, thin, high-heeled. Stocky, tough, seductive-scowled. Polo shirts. Glitter tees.

I grab Lindsay by the collar, pull her close enough to feel her heat, and say, "Take me home now."

I should have paused first, focused on my tone. I didn't mean to be gruff and full of rejection. I meant to be open, lightly floating an air of possibility between us. It came out all wrong and her brazen side quickly vanishes.

She whisks us home, the night air sharp and unforgiving. She apologizes at the front door, avoids my gaze. I am deflated. The rift of misunderstanding feels impossibly wide. Exhaustion closes in fast.

When I close the door, I've never felt more alone. Not even my mother has anything to say.

The new job isn't going well. I'm a paralegal, perpetual assistant to the lawyer set. I could spin a tale about how the work itself bores me, how I hate the deadlines and the dress code and the lunchtime cliques that never include me. But the bottom line is: I hate lawyers. I hate the way they will take absolutely anything—from the mundane to the obscene—and derive ridiculous pleasure out of building an argument for or against it. I hate the way their superiority so often hits their insecurity and turns into condescension. I hate their excessively dry-cleaned and pressed suits. I hate the overly important way they order coffee or stand at elevators. I hate the way they slip from casual indifference to intense concentration and you never know whether it's safe to say, "Good morning, Ms. O'Neil" or "Have a nice day, Counselor," without being in danger of receiving a curt, hurried reply.

I don't know why I thought any of this would be different in a different place. Too many cherished re-runs of "L.A. Law" in my childhood, I suppose. I'm crazy, but not crazy enough to think the problem is that I landed in San Diego and not Los Angeles. I will not move again. But the new job isn't going well.

In the morning, my head feels like a watermelon with a heartbeat, too heavy for my neck to support. Throbbing. I get a shower and decide that, starting today, I will dry up and shine like Southern California. To hell with everyone else. I will make my own happiness, thank you very much. I vacuum my living room, clean off the tables and counter tops, take three Hefty bags full of beer bottles and frozen food cartons out to the dumpster.

I load up the cooler with water and soda and head the SUV east, past Poway and Rancho Bernardo, winding through stony-peaked hilltops. I roll the window down, feeling the temperature fluctuate around corners, elevation trumping the bright orange sun, chilling my cheeks and fingertips. I head for the desert. Parched sand and uncluttered vistas. I want to see it all.

I make my way up the mountain roads to Julian, a former gold mining town now known for home-baked pies and eclectic crafts. I park in a gravel lot, do some deep knee bends, feel my waistband cutting my gut. I remember teenage summers in spandex and bikinis, long before I fell in love with vodka and Alfredo sauce in equal measure.

I see her sallow skin. Her sunken eyes. She's standing next to me, leaning against my dusty car-truck, a model she never glimpsed in her lifetime.

*You're lost*, she says.

I stroll the town of Julian. Buy wind chimes with a Wild West motif and a croissant at the bakery. I'm carefree, practically on vacation. I drive to a vista spot on Highway 79 just outside of town where you can see the Anza Borrego. Standing on the mountainside, I look down at the desert floor. Western skies are so big; it's disorienting to be able to see that far. It should make me feel small but it doesn't. Something about the endless sand and infinite sky makes me want to be a better person. Someone with the capacity to forgive, to connect again.

A family of four stands near the guardrail. Husband/father holds tightly onto his little girl's hand. Wife/mother clicks snapshots. Teenage son stares at his phone.

Daniel was from a big family. He wanted lots of kids. I was afraid. Always so goddamned afraid. My mother died when I was sixteen and despite all her efforts, I wasn't prepared. Wasn't ready.

The teenager walks back to the family sedan, opens the door. He glances down at his shoes, then up at me. His face is pale and unblemished. A single lock of black hair falls across his forehead. I feel a tiny shock, like static electricity in dry-heated winter.

I'm staring at the boy. He's staring at me. His hand is on the car door; he's not moving.

I'm fifteen and my mother's just told me. We're in the car, on our way to Key West. A vacation we deserved, she said. A vacation to remember. Staring out the bug-streaked windshield, she told me it was just a matter of time. She didn't cry or lose her winsome spirit. Every day holds infinite potential, she said. Every minute just as likely to explode into brilliance as fade into oblivion. In Key West, with grains of sand between her toes, tide rolling in, deep inhalations of salty ocean air, my mother lived a thousand years in a single afternoon.

Minutes. Seconds. So precious, she said.

*Live them.*

I feel the brisk hilltop breeze against my skin as I walk over, prop myself against the hood of the family's car, glance sideways at the teenager.

"Got a cigarette?" he says, fingers dangling out of his front jeans pockets, head slightly down.

"You shouldn't smoke," I say.

He shrugs, kicks at the gravel next to the curb.

"You been down there?" I ask, pointing at the desert.

"Too far, they keep saying. Not this time."

I breathe, and he breathes, and we watch the desert, from a distance.

His parents are thirty feet away, absorbed in their little girl, oblivious to this strange woman who has sauntered up to their son.

The boy is holding his phone, not looking at it. He's staring at the ground.

He's fifteen, maybe, tall and gangly, fresh from a hormone growth spurt. Only a foot from me now. I could reach out and touch his arm. The shock of electricity would jolt through me and buzz my senses from head to toe. I'd be able to recall that feeling, that intensity, at any moment in the future. It's palpable, already, and it hasn't even happened.

Maybe he's sixteen, I tell myself. Not a child.

A parent can die on you, boy. *Any minute now.*

He slips his phone into his pocket. As he moves, I catch a glimpse under his T-shirt, a thin strip of black hair just above the waistband of his jeans.

Are you going to talk to me now, Mother? Are you going to tell me to live this moment? I see the flare. It is *right here.*

The boy looks confused. He's backing away from me.

Did I say that out loud?

The boy's family approaches. Father wears a deep scowl. He's looking at his son; he's looking at me. "What are you doing?" he yells.

The boy gets in the car, doesn't look up. I don't exist. I was never here. I've never been anywhere. I grip the guardrail and look out. The man is behind me now. Car doors slam, the rest of the family tucking inside their Camry. I squat near the ground, clutch my knees.

"Are you okay, Miss?" the man says.

"Go away," I say.

"Are you sure? Do you need help?"

I am folding into myself. Can't hear anything but the wind. Nothing exists but the wind and the sky and the desert. The boy, the car, the family disappear. I don't look back. I will never see them again. Not in a thousand years. Ten thousand.

It's Wednesday afternoon and I'm back at the bar. This time I'm looking out the window. I'm watching the waves, seeing my mother in a rented convertible, boys on the beachfront strip whistling at her. She laughs, throws her head back. "Nothing to lose," she yells. "Nothing to lose!"

I tap my empty glass. Bartender pours me another.

"You all right, Sugar?" Her round face is kind, younger than I'd realized before.

"Sure," I say. "I'm fine."

After two more whiskeys, the bartender's wavy hair blurs with the beach beyond the window, darkening in the twilight. The jukebox volume rises over happy hour voices. People with jobs are mingling, grateful to be out for the day.

I lost my job two days before. I wish I cared.

My mother is sitting on the bar stool beside me. Wrinkles of concern, fraught with worry. I won't talk to her. I won't be that crazy woman anymore.

She sips her drink, which looks like soda, then says, "I've been watching you."

No shit, I think. You've been haunting me half my life. This is not news, Mother.

I drain my whiskey, stare back out the window. The dark edge of sunset. There are worse things to be than a drunk in Southern California.

"You don't look well." The background noise in the bar softens in time with her words. My vision clears for the tiniest interval.

Anger spins me around as Lindsay wrings her hands. "What are you, stalking me now?" I yell.

I ask for another drink.

"You driving her?" The bartender asks Lindsay.

"No, she's not," I say. "I don't need a ride. I need another drink, please—"

When I wake up I don't know where the hell I am. Lindsay is next to me, reading on an iPad.

"Good morning," she says, getting up. There's fear in her quick retreat. She knows I can hurt her in a heartbeat. Still, she's there, wearing that Mickey Mouse T-shirt and an apprehensive smile.

I roll over, feeling the discomfort of having slept fully clothed, chafed thighs and underarms.

My nightstand is by the bed. My dresser is in the corner. We are in my apartment. I have no memory of giving her my keys or allowing her in.

Through the shades, sunlight trickles across the wall. I squint as shadows form.

Teenage boys bumming cigarettes, watery-eyed and misunderstood.

They strut and breathe among rippled desert sand, atop stony mountains, at the crest of a wave crashing against rock and beach. It's not a dream. These California boys leaning against truck hoods and gazing at vistas, knowing they're connected to every prehistoric rock, every blade of grass. Their image rises as if to speak, not in my mother's voice, but painted in sunbeams on my apartment wall.

*You are alive*, the boys tell me. *Don't run away this time.*

Lindsay is standing at the door. "I should go," she says.

I hesitate, looking for the boys. The image is gone as quickly as it came.

Drawn to the window, I pull the shades up, let the light spill in. It's not like a flare at all. Not a revelation. But it's there, burning inside of my dry mouth.

Shaking, I turn to Lindsay. "I have nothing to offer you but grief," I say. "But stay with me awhile? It's possible I could use—a friend?"

Quickly, I need to sit down. To rest.

The room is utterly silent.

Slowly, Lindsay sits down beside me, gripping her hands, one over another.

Finally, she looks back up, and says, "I won't be your punching bag. If you want a friend, you have to be one. Can you do that?"

I feel the deep burrowing ache at the center of my chest. And with absolute certainty, I know my mother will never speak to me again. Whether I screw this up today or tomorrow or next year, she's done and gone. No more scolding. No more direction.

The lightness in the room is not from the Sun. It is me, wrapping my arm around Lindsay's shoulder, and saying, as softly as I can manage, "I can do that. And I will. I'm going to surprise the hell out of you."

# PHOTOPHOBIA

Darlene wore a gold cross on a chain, smoked unfiltered cigarettes, seldom made eye contact before noon. She said her father was a union man, laid off in '85, rarely sober since. I hired her for her looks and told her as much. That's the way it is, she said, grabbing my apron off the hook behind the bar. She hasn't missed a shift in two years. She knows I love her. Knows I'd slice open any man who crossed her if she wanted me to.

I was the sole proprietor of Lucky Jeb's Tavern, had been for sixteen years since my brother Jeb died. Couldn't see drunks stumbling into a place named Christina's at 10 a.m. for Wild Turkey and dusty peanuts so I never changed the name. Once, about six months after Darlene came on, I called the sign man and priced a pink neon "D." Told Darlene I'd name the place after her. She laughed and called me a horny old woman. Said lack of attention was making me queer and I needed to find a man, quit staring at her ass. That wasn't going to happen and we both knew it. Love doesn't tell your heart why. It just steps in, makes itself at home.

Darlene was legally blind though you'd never know it, except she couldn't drive. She was sharp behind the bar, never got an order wrong. Remembered the customers better than I did. Not driving posed some problems, though. Hitching with strangers was dangerous, I tried to tell her. Still, she did it all the time. No shortage of offers either. I put her on closing shifts, drove her home myself most nights.

Windows open in my Dodge four-wheeler while she smoked. Crickets growing louder as we got closer, her trailer set way back from the road. She lived with her old man in a double-wide on a twenty-acre plot. Her mother had fled to Oregon three years before. Darlene tried to do right by her father, though nothing worked. So she brought him a fresh bottle of whiskey every night and didn't hound him anymore.

I wished her sweet dreams. She peered in the open truck window, squinting. That pained look she got, wanting to see more clearly than her capabilities allowed.

"You're crazy," she said. Knocked twice on the truck door and walked away. Slower than usual. She stopped at the front door, one foot in, one out. Turned back and waved.

I held my hand up, expecting I was nothing but a blur of headlights to her, all white and glowing.

On a slow Tuesday night, tavern door propped open, inviting the clean March breeze inside. Two guys at the bar. I told Darlene I had it covered. She should rest awhile, watch a flick in my office.

She sat in my big brown recliner, took off her shoes, rubbed her toes, talked about her mother's corns and heel spurs. The dreaded fate of her feet. I brought her a fizzy Coke.

She touched my shirt sleeve, said it looked real nice.

"It's new," I said. Green cotton pullover, loose. I moved closer, to give her a better look.

Her hand grazed mine.

"You enjoy yourself tonight," I said. "Call me if you need anything."

I sat behind the bar, kept the whiskey levels rising for the regulars, glanced back at Darlene as often as I could. I didn't notice him come in, don't know how long he'd been there when he sat down in front of me, pushed his baseball cap back, and said, "Hey, darling. Remember me?"

Bucky Torrence, twisted grin and a brand new white shirt, fold creases still showing. My husband.

"Don't looked so shocked," he said. "Good behavior's my middle name. You know that."

Knot in my stomach, organs twisting around my spine.

"Long while since I had a visitor up there," Bucky said. "Something going on?"

Bucky eyed the men at the bar, touched the rim of his cap. My apron smelled of tobacco and sandalwood: Darlene. Sirens, loud voices, a tinny gun shot. The TV in my office.

"Come here," Bucky said.

The TV went silent.

"What's his name?" Bucky asked.

Darlene sidled up next to me, untied the apron around my waist, lifted it over my head. Bucky watched her. Tired restless eyes of a man who'd been in prison a very long time.

74

"This guy bothering you?" Darlene asked, her hand resting on my waist.

Bucky laughed, touched his face as if he were trying to remember who he was.

"This is my husband," I said. "Bucky, this is Darlene."

Darlene took the bottle of Jim Beam out of my hand, her face inches from mine, straining to read me. "I'll be right here," she said. "If you need anything."

"I'll take a beer," Bucky said, licking his lips.

Darlene pulled him a draft.

We took a booth near the back, Bucky acting like all the others, staring at my melancholy girl as she wiped down the bar. Her face softly tragic in repose, radiant when a quick smile overtook.

"She's young," he said.

"We need to talk." I cracked my knuckles, one by one, a nervous habit I hadn't exhibited in a decade.

"She living with you? You doing her?"

I looked at Darlene, then back to Bucky, my non-answer answering.

"Too bad," he said.

He laid his head down on the table. Those brown eyes. Delicate long lashes. Too delicate for a man, I always thought. His head rested on his muscled forearm.

"Take me home," he said. "Please."

"You can't expect that."

"'Til death do us part," he said. Deep crevices lined his forehead. His skin looked parched, achingly wind-blown.

Darlene wiped down tables with swift steady strokes of a dingy grey towel.

"A hot shower. Warm blanket on the sofa, a television I can leave on all night long," Bucky said. "You owe me that much, don't you?"

He sat up, pulled his cap down, drained his beer. "For all I've done for you."

I met Bucky Torrence in junior high. He was clunky, big, older than everyone else since they'd held him back three times. His dad worked with my uncle at the auto shop; his family was always good friends with mine. Barbeques in the backyard, tractor pulls, rodeos. Bucky was always around. He called me Prissy Chrissy one year, said I was the most beautiful girl he'd ever seen the next. I was a brute and a tomboy and that never changed.

Bucky didn't care. He took me to the prom, gave me Valentine hearts. Only boy who ever showed any interest at all.

He proposed in the back seat of his father's rusty Cadillac, my pants around my ankles. Go ahead, I told him, just do it. Take my virginity and stop begging. He stopped short, zipped his pants up, and said he loved me. Pulled out a ring with the tiniest diamond I'd ever seen and asked me to marry him.

He was the stupidest boy I'd ever known, but I said yes. My bare ass freezing on those fake leather seats, I said yes, I would marry him. I was eighteen and didn't know a damn thing about who I was or what I would become. But Bucky loved me; he'd do anything I asked him to do. And that was something.

Bucky fell asleep in the brown recliner in my office, TV blaring beside him. The last patron of the night was Sam Grinnell, a divorced insurance salesman with twin teenage girls his ex-wife carted off to Texas.

Darlene coaxed Sam toward the door.

Sam pushed his phone towards Darlene. A picture of his twins in matching softball uniforms. "Julie's quite the hitter this year," Sam said. "Did I show you the clip of her home run?"

"You did," Darlene said. "Two times."

Sam bumped into a chair, caught himself. "One more drink. I could really use one more—"

"Not tonight," I said.

Darlene held the door open.

"That guy—" Sam nodded toward the office. "A bit shady, isn't he?"

"My ex," I said.

Sam stood straight up. "Ex-what?"

"We're fine," I said. "You be careful getting home now."

Sam lived two doors down in a crappy apartment above the Chinese place. Still, I worried he might stumble and crack his skull on the pavement.

He smoothed his wrinkled shirt down, said, "Good night, ladies."

I dropped ice cubes in two tumblers, poured the best vodka I had. Pushed one across the bar to Darlene.

"You know I don't," she said.

I downed mine. Took hers, too.

She joined me behind the bar, laid her hand on my forearm. So many times I'd dreamed of her next to me, closer than close. Now there she was.

"It's okay," I said. "I'm fine."

"Why didn't I know this?"

"Doesn't matter."

Darlene draped her arm around my shoulder, abandoning her usual reluctance. She stood flush against me, caressed the back of my neck with her fingertips. Whispered my name.

"I'll take you home," I said. "Like always."

"Is he dangerous? What'd he do?"

"Don't ask," I said.

"Tina—"

"I can handle him."

"Jesus, Christina, tell me."

The television went silent in the other room.

Bucky wobbled out, his face thick with black stubble, his eyes red-lined and watery. "You got a pistol behind that bar, baby?" he asked.

Darlene straightened her spine. I moved around her.

"Darlene needs a ride. There's only room for two in the truck."

"Fuck that. We can squeeze in the cab."

I drove and Darlene pressed in next to me, her thigh touching mine as she inched away from Bucky on the other side. I wanted to get her home as fast as possible but something pulled me in the other direction. I turned left where I should have turned right. Darlene couldn't see well enough to know.

The thick night steamed the air. Radio cackled below the cricket and bullfrog chorus.

Bucky draped his arm around Darlene, splayed his legs wide. "Beautiful night. Beautiful woman next to me. Shit, I'm a lucky man," he said.

He laughed hard, until he was choking. Coughing. Clutching at Darlene. "Oh yes, I'm lucky all right. Fifteen years lucky. Right, baby?"

"Buck—"

"Damn sight luckier than ol' Jeb though. Poor ol' fucked up Brother Jeb."

"Stop it," I said. "Just stop."

"Oh, come on, baby. You haven't told your girlfriend about Lucky Jeb?"

I made another wrong turn, twisting around the dark side of the park.

"Where are we?" Darlene whispered in my direction.

I bit my lip. Realized she couldn't read my face.

Bucky leaned in close to Darlene. "What's this?" he said, pulling her father's nightly bottle from between her legs. "Who you got waiting at home? Boyfriend? Husband? A *woman*?"

He cracked open the bottle, took a long swallow.

Another.

He gripped my shoulder. "This girl wants to party. Been staring at me all night. Turn this fucker around. We're taking her home with us," he said. "I got this coming, Chrissy. You have to admit."

Bucky pulled Darlene toward him. She kicked at him, thrashed. He didn't let go. They struggled and I swerved the truck across the center line, clenched my right fist, threw a punch without looking. Got Bucky in the side of the face, hard. Knuckles into his cheek, jagged silver ring slicing his skin.

"Goddamnit," he said, and gripped Darlene again. He ripped at her shirt, pulled it off with one fast motion down.

I let go of the steering wheel, reached for the blade tucked in my boot heel. The truck lurched into the ditch and Bucky lost his grip on Darlene. She fell against me. I stood, somehow sideways on the brake, the blade in my hand coming down, into Bucky's shoulder. It happened so fast, Darlene slipped behind me. The truck rocked, back and forth. Bucky knocked the knife from my hand. Yelling and thrashing as the truck stopped. Stood still. I pounded my fist into Bucky's wound. Blood everywhere. He gripped my shoulders, shaking me. He was big—huge—no way to overpower him. His hands on my throat. Squeezing. Then, from nowhere, he gasped, let me go, his eyes bulging.

Darlene. Knife in her hand. She sliced into his abdomen. Again and again and again. Blood spilling, from his gut and his mouth. His gaze went steady.

Quiet. So thick and quiet I couldn't breathe.

Darlene tugged, pushed me out of the truck and we were running. Heavy air, humid as July though I knew it was March. Almost spring, I thought. The flowers would bloom soon. I ran behind Darlene into the thick black woods, thinking of red and yellow tulips. How they unfold themselves to the sun, open so wide, so uninhibited. They crave the heat, source of energy and life. Yet when darkness falls and the day turns quiet and cold, tulips fold themselves in, waiting for their warm sun to return.

We didn't stop until the clearing, until we were standing in the spray of the back porch light behind the trailer. Sweat glistened off Darlene's bare skin; it was caked in her hair. Jeans and a lace bra, her shirt lost in the truck cab. On the floorboard of my truck. Next to my dead husband. Next to Bucky's lifeless feet. His leather boots and the blade I knew was there, but he'd never pulled.

"We have to get out of here. Have to find a way out," Darlene said.

"No," I said. "I know what to do."

We sat at the dinette table, brand new bottle of whiskey and four hands. Quiet and still. Darlene's father snored in the next room. I'm not crazy and I'm no fool, but I knew I was right and finally, I convinced her. To let me call the police.

When I hung up, Darlene poured the whiskey, drank two shots without pause.

"Not a good idea," I said. "Detective will be here shortly."

She paced back and forth, trembling.

"You're sure about this?"

"Certain," I said. "Don't worry."

It played out as I told her it would. Bucky was just released from prison, believed by all to be a violent man. He'd threatened Darlene, then attacked her.

Self-defense. Justified.

The detective was a Lucky Jeb regular. I poured him a drink and he took our story down on a small yellow pad.

"Bucky was upstate a long time," he said. "Buddy of mine's a guard up there. Said he had it in for you real bad, Tina. We should've had some protection down at the Tavern tonight. Real sorry about that, I am."

He patted Darlene's arm. "You okay?"

She nodded.

I took the detective's place on the sofa when he was gone. Light filtered in through half-closed blinds, stripes of dawn creeping in. Darlene rubbed her eyes.

"He was your husband," she said.

I kissed her shoulder, touched the side of her face.

"Tell me about Lucky Jeb," she said.

So I told her. My brother Jeb was murdered. No one talked about it at the bar because that's the way I liked it, and they knew better than to cross me. Case went unsolved for months. Jeb's wife disappeared, never heard from again. More evidence came out; there'd been a love triangle. Things pointed to a jealous lover. The wife's lover, but the case was weak. They convicted Bucky. Manslaughter.

Darlene looked out the window and didn't ask questions. Not even the obvious ones I feared most. Sun spilled in the room, and the lines in her face seemed to deepen. Sink. She struggled to see me clearly but I knew she couldn't. All that light and her poor eyes. I knew it hurt her just to try.

"I love you, Darlene. Close your eyes. Rest."

Her father still slept in the bedroom, just a few feet away. My first time in their trailer but you'd never know it. My shoulders relaxed and I exhaled. I touched Darlene's hair, ran my finger down the side of her face, her neck.

She flinched. Squinted at me.

I'd told her the story and I didn't lie. A killer in love doesn't tell everything; she just slips in, makes herself at home.

# PHANTOM ADVANCES

My mother lost her job on a cold Friday in January and decided it was the perfect excuse to go on vacation. She'd been working so hard. Late hours, Saturdays too. The freight company she'd been with since last summer lost its government contract, had to scale back. She told me this as soon as I walked in the door, not even a chance to drop my books on the table and get a Coke from the fridge.

My mind lept to the rent. Our landlord was a simple guy and crushed out on Mom big time, but he wasn't fool enough to let us ride rent-free. I'd been mowing lawns for him, had $400 hidden in an old sneaker in my closet. I never spent much money. Junk from 7-Eleven, the occasional used paperback. Tucked the rest in my shoe.

"I say we fill up the tank and drive to North Carolina," Mom said.

"What about school?"

"You can miss a few days. It bores you to tears. Isn't that what you say?"

I shrugged.

"You haven't seen your grandparents in over a year."

Her large suitcase sat in the corner, packed and waiting for me to lug it out to the car. There was a cooler on the kitchen counter, already full of ice, Cokes, ham sandwiches.

"We're leaving tonight?" I asked.

Mom bounced off the sofa and threw her arms around my neck. "Oh, Allie! I knew you'd be up for it!"

She pulled her hair back with a rubber band, her road-warrior look. Her voice had kicked into its sing-songy don't-bother-me-with-reality tone. I didn't ask how much money there was in the checking account. Didn't ask how long we were going to be gone.

I tucked four paperbacks into my suitcase, two I hadn't read and two I had. With advance warning I would have made a special trip to the library, selected a stack of Stephen King or Robert Heinlein for the trip. There was no time for that.

We passed the state line into Georgia just after 9 p.m.

Mom kept playing the same Carly Simon cassette tape over and over, saying how great it was to get away, how exciting to just take off. Maybe we'll never go back, she said. What if we disappeared and never saw anyone we knew ever again?

My mother poured herself into things then erased them just as fast, as if they'd never existed at all. I always dug for the foundation, searching for the anchor. We were so different; I imagined myself a freak of genetic mutation. But I only knew half my equation. My father was the mystery I'd been trying to solve since I was old enough to talk. He died when I was two. An accident, Mom said. A car, too much alcohol, a telephone pole. I didn't know much more than that about him. My questions went unanswered. Subject always changed.

Near midnight, South Carolina was indistinguishable from Georgia, a continuous tunnel of gloomy darkness sprinkled with streams of white light coming toward us, glowing red specks fading behind.

I thought about the things I'd miss at school the next week. It was fine with me if I never returned to Edgewood High but Mom knew better than to steal a Learning Center Friday from me, or I hoped she did. This year my Fridays belonged to Nietzsche, Tennessee Williams, and Ansel Adams: my reward for living with the label "gifted."

Mom sipped coffee out of an insulated mug, tapping her rings on the steering wheel. She was determined to drive straight through, put us into Maynard by late afternoon. I wanted to sleep but I was afraid Mom's caffeine would wear off, the music would mellow her mood, and we'd end up either in the ditch or speeding across the median.

"Why North Carolina?" I asked.

"What?" She turned the music down.

"Why North Carolina?" I said.

"That's where they are."

"But you never want to go. We only went last time because Granpa broke his leg."

I watched her profile in the glow of the dashboard lights and felt a quick stab of pain, right in the center of my chest. Was someone sick? Or worse? It would be just like her to wait until the North Carolina Welcome Center to mention Granma was dead. Or Aunt Cindy'd had a stroke.

"I thought it would be fun," she said. "Just us girls on a road trip. Spur of the moment. A respite from everyday."

"Is anyone dead?"

"Allie!"

"I'm serious. Are Granma and Granpa okay?"

"They're fine! Well, I assume they're fine. I haven't talked to them in weeks."

I leaned my head back against the vinyl seat, propped my knees against the dashboard.

"Jeez, honey. Why would you say that?"

I pulled a pack of bubble gum out of my pocket, offered her one. We blew bubbles in unison. I turned Carly Simon back up just as the first drops of rain hit the windshield.

It rained all night and the roads became treacherous. We pulled over to wait it out just past Florence. I was so tired I could barely keep focused. There was a fuzzy white halo at the edge of my vision. I blinked and shook my head. It just got blurrier, water cascading down the windshield. Mom was staring straight ahead, not blinking. It was 3:30 in the morning and I'd been awake for twenty-one hours. I didn't know how she was holding her eyes open.

"You okay?" I said.

There was mist at the corner of her eyes. I wished I could force myself into wakefulness. Mom looked scared or lonely or afraid. I couldn't distinguish through my blurriness and the hypnotic sound of the pouring rain, encircling and concealing.

"Close your eyes awhile," she said. "You look horrible."

I laid my seat back and curled up.

We pulled the Plymouth into the gravel and grass driveway and there was Granpa on the front porch. It was dusk and the porch light was on; yellow and brown leaves blanketed the yard. Granpa folded the newspaper, stood up, yelled something toward the house.

My mother grabbed my arm. "Let's not—"

"I know."

"It's just a vacation. No reason."

"Right."

Mom didn't have the best track record with employment. She wasn't lazy and she wasn't stupid; in fact, it was the opposite. She was hard-working and bright, but she had a certain intensity that didn't play well in the typing pool or behind a receptionist's desk. She should have gone to college; she could have been a doctor, lawyer, Wall Street broker. Instead, she had me.

We would tell my grandparents Mom's job was going well, everyone at the office loved her and she'd just received a raise, been given a week's vacation as special thanks for all her hard work. She told that entire story to Granpa before our suitcases were even out of the trunk. My mother's father was a grey man from head to toe, disheveled hair and stubble in random splotches. He wore grey trousers and a grey sweatshirt and his white-gold wedding band blended right into his ashen skin. He looked skeptical of Mom's enthusiastic tale, but his reluctant, shy grin pinkened his cheeks when he hugged us hello.

Upstairs, I splashed water on my face, stared into the mirror at the purple lines under my eyes. I loved my grandparents and I was happy to see them, but the infrequency of our visits forced tension into the smallest details. Mom would try to pull me into her fortress of denied reality, and every lie felt like a tiny stress fracture. There was only so far I was willing to stray from the truth. Even for her.

Downstairs, Granma fed us Campbell's soup and saltines and Mom talked non-stop. About the rain. About the 18-wheeler that nearly ran us off the road in Jacksonville. She told lies about my alcoholic uncle, her brother. Stories about a job he didn't have, girlfriends who adored him, cooked for him, fought over his affection. When it was clear my grandparents wouldn't contribute to Mom's fantasy life of their depressed and damaged son, the subject turned to me. My perfect grades and astonishing genius. The new gifted program at The Learning Center.

Granma crumpled crackers into her soup and we both watched Mom talking so fast she grew breathless. When she paused to take a sip of water, Granma touched my arm, and said, "Now that you're older, do you still enjoy mathematics, Allie?"

I tried not to make eye contact with Mom. She'd been obsessed with my mathematical talents ever since I was a child and the teachers declared me some kind of calculating prodigy. The truth was I'd always hated knowing the answers without having to try. I wasn't a genius; I was a freak. I hated math.

But Mom didn't want me to tell Granma the truth. This was not the place to reveal our disappointments and weaknesses, she would say. No one needs to know those things.

Granma was looking straight at me, so sincere and interested.

"No," I said. "I don't enjoy it."

Mom gripped her fork, hard.

Granpa was lost in a daydream. He was off fishing or hunting in his mind, I imagined. He was a simple man. Quiet and unconcerned.

Granma, on the other hand, was forthright and smart and a college graduate. Though she never utilized her history degree in a career, she read the newspaper cover-to-cover every day and she could talk for hours about capitalism and communism and the true nature of democracy.

"What do you enjoy, then?" Granma asked, holding a saltine between two fingers, pinkie extended in a genteel Southern gesture that looked so natural for her yet would have been laughable if Mom or I had tried it.

"I like Nietzsche, and black-and-white photography," I said.

"Nietzsche?"

"German philosopher."

"I know who he is, dear."

I finished my soup and watched Granma. She looked puzzled, as if she were straining to recall something distant and unpleasant.

"Will to power. The Übermensch," she finally said. "Do you know about the connection between Hitler and *Mein Kampf?*"

My mother kicked me under the table. "Allie scored a 145 on her IQ test. Can you believe that, Dad? 145!"

Granpa sipped his soup without looking at anyone.

"Nietzsche's work was apolitical." I said. "Hitler didn't understand it."

"'Politics is for the moment. An equation is for eternity.' Do you know that quote, Allie?" Granma asked.

"Einstein," I said.

Granma smiled. Mom got up to clear the table. She took my bowl, which was still half full of soup. She'd washed it, dried it, and it was on the way to the cupboard before she noticed we were all staring at her.

My grandfather was a career soldier. He joined the Army during the war to fight Hitler and the Japanese Imperialists, as Granma always described. He served in the Pacific theater, brought home two purple hearts. Granma showed them to me once in a hand-carved wooden box. His platoon was hit by Japanese jets dropping bombs from the sky; Granpa never wanted to talk about it. After the war, he worked as an engineering technician in Georgia, Ohio, and finally North Carolina. He retired with the rank of Chief Warrant Officer.

Two of Granma's brothers fought in the war too. Neither of them made it home alive. I knew more about my two great uncles who died almost twenty-five years before I was born than I knew about my own father. I used to get angry about that. Once I even wished my father had gone to Vietnam and died there, thinking in my childish way that death in the name of service and country was what released my grandmother's cherished memories of her brothers and allowed them to be shared. If only my father had died in a war, maybe my mother would have told me what I desperately longed to know.

The next morning I slept until almost noon. I woke smelling coffee. Downstairs, my mother peeled potatoes and talked about taking a side trip to the Outer Banks. "To look at the ocean."

Granma sat at the kitchen table in her housecoat, sipping coffee, and reading the obituaries.

"It's too cold for the beach," I said.

Granma folded the newspaper over.

"We don't have to go in the water," Mom said. "Just take a ride."

It was five more hours of driving each way. I didn't want to go, but there was no point in arguing with Mom once she'd made up her mind.

"There's Corn Flakes in the cupboard and bread for toast," Granma said. "Eat before you go."

Mom grabbed me into a hug and squeezed. She kissed my cheek and her fingertips pressed hard into my sides. When she finally let go, she said, "I'll make you eggs."

Mom drove so fast we got to Kitty Hawk in only four hours. I kept my nose in *A Separate Peace* and tried to tune out Carly Simon on heavy rotation again.

It was windy and cold on the beach, as I'd feared. We bundled into jackets, forced our hands deep into our pockets. We watched the waves, reached down to touch the sand, the coarse grains offering solace to things unnamed and unexplored.

We ate fried seafood at a beachfront dive with a small fireplace and pictures of the Wright Brothers. I watched Mom dip shrimp into the spicy cocktail sauce and puzzled over how she could look so lost and so beautiful at the same time. Her eyes drifted between here and not-here so quickly it made me dizzy, left me feeling alone.

"I came here with your father once," she said.

I stopped chewing. "Here? To this restaurant?"

She looked out the window toward the beach. The misty white halo returned at the corners of my vision but it wasn't from lack of sleep or forced waking. I gripped the sides of my chair with my fingertips, tried to decide what to say, how to get her to talk and not shut back down. To tell me a story I'd never heard before. About her and my father. Something they shared, something they did, what he was like, what she was like, who they were, and who that made me.

"No," she said. "To the beach."

"When? Was I there?"

"No," she said. "Before."

She wouldn't look at me. I wanted her to take my hands and look me in the eye. Tell me my father was a good man. That he was kind and warm. She never said that. At night when I couldn't sleep, I told myself she didn't say those things because it hurt too much. That remembering him made it worse and she wasn't as strong or as stoic as she wanted me to believe. But I didn't know. He was a mystery, and the clues, the secrets, the answers lived sealed up inside my mother.

"He was a strong swimmer," she said.

I held my breath.

"Very strong."

The waiter came and refilled our drinks. My mother's glassy stare faded away as she smiled, and said, "Thank you."

I asked questions. I tried to steer her back, but she was done. The glimpse of memory, the hope of revelation, extinguished. She ate her last shrimp, wiped her mouth on the little paper napkin, and folded my father back inside of herself.

"Let's go," she said. "Long drive."

We drove back to Maynard in silence. No music, no discussion. I stared out the window. I would have screamed if it would have helped. But that's not what I wanted. As angry as I was with her silence, these moments were so rare that when they came, I cherished them.

My father was a strong swimmer. My parents went to Kitty Hawk together. I could see them walking hand in hand on the beach.

I turned away from Mom. My lip quivered.

After three days of saying nothing more than good morning and good night, my grandfather touched my shoulder after breakfast, and said, "Something to show you."

I followed him down to what looked like a tool shed. When he opened the door and pulled the string on the light bulb overhead, he revealed an entire artist's studio full of paints, easels, and contraptions molded out of clay. The room was only a hundred square feet but it was lined with shelves, floor to ceiling, stocked with buckets and brushes and canvases. It was astonishing, to open a door and see someone you loved in an entirely new way. Everything I knew about my grandfather changed in that moment. As if he were someone else now, a stranger. Yet still, the same.

He walked to a small table, and said, "You like photography."

"I'm taking a class," I said. "Black and white."

"You have a camera?"

He knew Mom couldn't afford it. Turning around, he held out a smallish 35mm, a Pentax K-1000.

"I bought this a year or so ago, but it doesn't suit me," he said.

He placed the camera in my hands, weighty and solid. I held it up, set my eye against the viewfinder. Perfect.

"No film in it," he said.

I pressed the silver button, the aperture shut and released, the mechanical sound triggering something in my own eye. I felt it ripple across my skin, across my fingers, burrowing into my nail bed. There was Granpa through the viewfinder, as I'd never seen him before. Fragile and rugged, a tall, quiet artist. He looked back at me through the lens, and said, "You're a natural."

My face flushed. I suspected he'd bought the camera the day before, not a year. That he'd bought it for me. Never commenting on photography at the dinner table or asking me to elaborate on my interest. He just took note and made the purchase.

I held the camera close and thanked him. I stepped toward a set of canvases propped against the far wall while Granpa dug around in a bucket of paintbrushes, as if he were looking for something he desperately needed to find. I wondered what captivated his artist's heart. What was his cherished subject? I imagined a barren or rugged landscape. A faded orange sunset over mountains or ocean. But just as my fingers found the edge of one of his paintings, Granpa flipped off the light and nudged me gently out the door. He'd let me into his private world for long enough. There wasn't enough time to see it all clearly. I couldn't reproduce or describe it in detail, but as I stepped outside with his warm palm on my shoulder, I knew in my one fleeting glimpse of his painting, what I'd seen was a troubled young man's face.

I told my mother nothing more than what Granpa had told me. That it was an old camera he didn't want. But I knew a few things about the Pentax K-1000. It was perfect for a beginner. Basic. Solid. Full manual functionality without any excess. Whether it was true or not, I told myself he bought it just for me. That it was something special, a gift from one secret artist to another. And when I picked it up and put my eye to the viewfinder, I saw my grandfather in his cramped but luminous tool shed studio, painting faces he would never let me see.

I convinced Mom to leave before dawn on Thursday, to get us home in time for The Learning Center on Friday. I was carrying my bag down the steep wooden staircase, not fully awake yet. I stopped, instinctively, when I heard crying. I took one more step. My mother and Granma stood at the edge of the living room, wrapped in each other's arms. Mom was sobbing. I clutched my bag and tried not to make a sound. I watched the two of them, in a moment of purely expressed emotion. An event so rare in my family I lost my breath. A cough tickled at the back of my tongue and I struggled to suppress it, watching my grandmother stroke my mother's hair, kiss her forehead.

An envelope passed from Granma to my mother and I knew why we'd come to North Carolina. Our finances were worse than I thought, and my mother had spoken the truth, in the quiet of the early morning, to her mother and no one else.

After the envelope was tucked into Mom's pocket, she ran her hands through her hair and her sing-songy voice kicked in again, saying we needed to get going. We had a long drive ahead of us.

I continued downstairs, took my bag out the front door.

The bright sun reflected off the streaks in the windshield. I picked up my new camera, steadied it against my face, practiced the simultaneous squinting of the left eye, intense concentration of the right. I focused on my mother's profile. At first she laughed, stuck her tongue out, held her hand up to block my view. I stayed with it. Kept watching. No film there to record the moments. Just false clicks. Phantom advances. Somewhere in Georgia, Mom's jaw muscles loosened and the pain behind her eyes began to retreat. She didn't deflect my attention with a joke. For a few seconds, she was present. I didn't click, didn't shoot. I stayed there, my eye behind the viewfinder, knowing I'd slipped into her private space but it wouldn't be for long. Soon she'd nudge me away, and we'd be home.

# DOWNTOWN

The boys are stoned again and that means pizza. We trek ten blocks down to the tiny place on 68th. An Armenian soap opera is playing on the screen suspended above the counter. The sound is full of static and the acting is at least two notches worse than the Mexican soaps that play all night at the laundromat.

Cheese, cheese, extra, extra, says Peter. Pepperoni for Kenny. I sliver around the front table. Tuck myself into the windowsill, sit with knees pretzeled. Thin, light, barely there, I lay my head against the cool concrete wall, feel its depressions against my brow. A stream of taxis pours down Columbus Avenue. It's dusk and headlights flip on, two by two, cabs trolling for fares heading downtown. River of lights, constantly flowing.

A guy sits on the street corner across from the pizza place, next to the ATMs. He holds a cardboard sign that says "Need money for beer." A woman pushes a double-wide stroller past him, shakes her head. Twins. A boy and a girl, side-by-side, tiny hands reaching for the other's. I want to press my forehead against each of the babies'; I want to hear their secret language. They would never let me in; my brother Tag and I never let anyone in. A man in a pink tie tosses a dollar.

Tag and I moved to Manhattan three years ago. He took the lower quadrant, East Village, and I claimed the Upper West Side, spreading our inheritance across the island, a desperate salve that healed nothing. He lived in a loft on St. Mark's with great morning sun, where he painted and drank. Neither of us needed jobs, but he took one at a gallery, installing other people's art. I went to auditions, never ate, and started screwing Kenny. Because he was always there, as close as family, yet not. I stood up my therapist every other week.

Tag used to call me in the middle of the night. "What do you hear out your window?" he'd say.

I'd tell him about the birds. So many birds, singing—loud—at all hours of the day. Songbirds, chirping birds, squawking birds, illogically drowning out all the other city sounds. Tag held the phone up to his window, letting me hear the East Village.

Music, the clinking of glasses, laughter.

"I never sleep," he said.

Jumbo triangles of pizza on paper plates. The boys flop in plastic chairs. I pull my legs together. I'm still wearing my black nylons even though Kenny scraped the hell out of them that morning in the alley off 79th. "Can't wait," he said. "Can't."

Kenny is beautiful in the way only boys can be beautiful. Deep dark eyes and thick lashes. He was my brother Tag's best friend. He says being with me is almost consolation.

Kenny and Peter and I have lived this way for nine months now. We do the same things; we make each other crazy. We got into a cab once, about two months ago, and I said, "St. Mark's" before I realized. Peter and I were paralyzed. Kenny corrected our course, telling the driver, "Columbus Circle. Stop there."

Kenny eats his pizza backwards, crust first. He rolls the rest into a ball and nibbles it like a rabbit. Peter fills the air with that high, raucous laugh that means nothing.

In junior high, Peter was a track star, a middle-distance runner with a smooth, agile stride. He was in our class yet younger by two years. Tag, the magnetic field of misfits, brought him into our orbit.

"He's a genius," Tag said. "Geniuses are fragile because they know too much. That makes them beautiful, too."

In high school, Peter carried a small notebook, scribbling ideas and stolen bits of dialogue. He loved to recite Tennessee Williams. His own plays were philosophical rants with wild emotional swings, perfect for highlighting an actor's sensitivity and depth. He produced Kenny's first showcase in the city. Mine, too.

Tag was in love from the start. He waited until Peter was seventeen to seduce him. I never thought of them as permanent or serious. But loss can magnify devotion and I respect that. Grieving Tag is not a contest. The three of us are comrades, not competitors. We exist in antagonistic symbiosis. We don't talk about it. We've never been able to find the words.

In the pizza place, I look through the boys the way they look through me. They never ask if I want to eat because I always say no. My stomach is a clenched fist. There are two women sitting at the far back table. One is round-faced and wears a man's long-sleeve shirt. Oxford, button-down. Her hair is cut short, clean, part on the side, the way Tag used to wear his. The other woman is tall and slim. She wraps an orange shawl around her shoulders. She moves like the famous. I don't recognize her, yet I think I should; I want to know what roles she's played, what stage she commands. She leans forward and says something I can't hear. The other tucks her head into her shoulder, and blushes. The tall one takes the other's fingers into her hands, kisses them slowly. I imagine the two of them in a sun-filled apartment, making love all morning and into the afternoon. They both wear a glassy-eyed daze, as if that's exactly where they'd been. I imagine them under a pile of soft blankets, taking solace in the brush of smooth skin.

They are not young women. They have wrinkles and laugh lines and they are feeding each other pizza. The tall one places her hand against her lover's face. They stare into each others' eyes. The shawl falls off the woman's shoulder. She turns her body slightly away, reaches into her bag, pulls out a cell phone. Her expression clouds.

The sky is dark now. The city lights flicker white, red.

We missed the Improvisation Workshop again. None of us have had an audition in months. In the afternoon, we fell asleep on the rocks in the park until the ballfields crawled with kids after school, their shrill voices echoing off the jagged, cold stone. Peter woke up swearing at the kids, the sun, dogs barking, Kenny.

"Where's the shit? Give me the shit!"

Kenny's chin dug into my side and I felt a little sick, while Peter kept yelling. "Gimme the shit. Where's the shit?"

Kenny pulled out the bag, handed it to him. "Not here."

We stopped near the wall by the playground where the foliage is thick. I strained to hear a chorus of invisible birds while the two of them finished off our weed. My eyes closed, I tried to conjure Tag's voice, his smile. My memories are jagged and rough. I would force them if I could, rip them through muscle and bone.

Now Peter is shoving an entire slice of pizza into his mouth, folded over. Grease drips down his chin. His blond hair is clumped and dirty, his shirt buttoned askew. I wonder how long it's been since he went home to his mother and three little sisters in Brooklyn who adore him. His family is alive and they love him, yet here he is, with us. I want to push him out the door, tell him to grow up. To move on. Before I can, Peter jumps out of his chair, yelling, "I'm wet. Wet. Everywhere wet!"

He pushes Kenny, sends him rocking against the table. "Did you spill something on me? Where did it come from?"

Kenny's in a daze. He's farther away than I am.

When we were kids, Kenny had a red bicycle with white rim tires. He rode it up and down the block, as slow as he could without stopping, steering with one finger. Tag and I watched from our front stoop as he rode back and forth. Entire lifetimes pass on front stoops in Brooklyn.

Tag leaned into me once, whispered, "James Dean's Schwinn."

Remembering this, I laugh out loud. Peter spins around. "Why do you always take *his* goddamned side?"

Peter hates me for reasons he doesn't understand. The instinct is buried deep in his limbic system. Yet there are times when he can't take his eyes off me. He searches for Tag in my face, without apology. I don't blame him. I do it sometimes too. In the mirror.

On the screen above our heads, a woman with enormous breasts is weeping. Her chest heaves, and Kenny smirks.

Peter pulls a quarter out of his pocket, rubs it down his pant leg. "It's wet. Feel—"

He presses the coin against Kenny's arm. "Feel!" he says, grabbing Kenny's hand.

Kenny brushes him off. "Don't touch me, Fruit Loop. You're wasted. Eat more pizza."

The two women in the back are looking at us. The round-faced one catches my eye. She's boyish and plain, and I'm filled with a strange urgency to know her name. She's not intriguing in the way of her elegant lover. But I want to name them both.

Tag and Katrina. He called me Kat. No one else but Tag called me Kat.

"I'm leaking," Peter says. "I'm leaking out of my pores."

I press my forehead against the window. Its panes are double thick. The women are in my peripheral vision. The tall one stares at Kenny. Her brow is furrowed, as if she's puzzling out an equation. Kenny gets out of his chair, grips Peter's shoulders.

"You're dry as a bone," he says. "I wouldn't lie to you. Okay?"

"You can't feel it? You really can't?" Peter says.

I'm afraid he's going to cry. It happens sometimes.

The guys behind the pizza counter nudge each other. The Armenian soap opera goes to commercial. They mute it.

Kenny puts his arm around Peter. "Another slice?"

A cell phone rings, loud enough to turn everyone's head. One of those ear-piercing classic-phone ring tones, as if we're sitting in a 1970s trailer park in Florida or Arizona. That sound doesn't belong here. It's an aberration.

The tall woman clutches the ringing beast to her chest. Briskly, she heads toward our table, the door, the street. Her face is sliced with harsh angles. Her voice, deep and frazzled, answers: "Meeting went long. Leaving work right now. Yes. Yes. I'm on my way."

She barely makes it out the door, then she's back, tucking the phone in the pocket of her snug jeans. She tilts her head up. Her lips are moving but she's not speaking. She's calculating something, counting—1, 2, 3—as she returns to the table where the lover is waiting.

Peter is still mumbling, "Wet, wet, wet," as if he were the only unstable boy in the world.

Between a paper plate and a Coke can, four hands entwine on the women's table. No words. No more smiles. The tall one stands up again, wraps her shawl across her body, loops her bag over her shoulder. She walks trash to the dispenser. The other slips in beside her, compliant. Her shape isn't as boyish as her haircut and face. Her shirt is tucked neatly into black trousers. Her curves are not hidden, hips not shy. The two women melt into one another, navigating the small space without letting go.

The pizza counter guys watch them. Kenny watches, too.

I start to stand up. Stop halfway, sitting on the table like a centerpiece at Thanksgiving. I reach for Kenny; Kenny holds onto Peter. As the women brush past, holding hands—for a fraction of a second—we're a human chain, connected. Me, Kenny, Peter, the tall woman, and her lover. As they leave, the two women grapple closer. They would occupy the same skin if they could; I can feel it.

When they're gone, the fist in my stomach tightens. Out the window, I see them kiss on Columbus Avenue. The tall woman hails a cab, gets in alone. The other buries her hands in her pockets. She doesn't move for a long time.

Taillights, people, billboards on buses.

The woman left behind stands on the curb.

No one knows what my brother Tag meant to me. No one knows who we were to each other. Fraternal means less, they say. Two eggs and two sperm. Just siblings born on the same day.

Biology tells us nothing about the soul. There is no explanation for connection. Or desire.

Kenny was Tag's best friend. Peter was his lover for years. Neither of them had any idea who Tag and I really were to each other. They still don't.

Peter sits down, takes a sip of his soda, and tells Kenny: "I want something. Call Javier."

The sound returns on the TV; the channel is switched to soccer.

Kenny pulls out his cell, begins thumbing out a text.

I look back out the window. The woman is no longer there.

Does she live in the city? Does she go back to an apartment, or a hotel. When will the lovers meet again? How deep do their secrets go? Does anyone know who they are to each other. How will it end?

Kenny smells of sweat and pepperoni. Into his ear, I whisper, "Downtown."

He stops typing, studies Peter's face for a long beat, says, "Not ready."

Peter finishes his soda, and chants: "Javier. Javier."

I wrap my arms around Kenny's neck. He lifts me off the table. I am a feather. A fleck of dust. Confetti.

"Tonight," I whisper.

He pretends not to hear.

The air is stale with exhaust and garbage. Oily green residue lines the sidewalk. Kenny and I step around it; Peter walks right through.

Kenny's cell phone vibrates. His voice notches up an octave. "Javier's holding, up on 93rd."

"Yes," says Peter, "All right." He's already walking.

"I'm going," I say. "Right now."

I stop where the two women parted. The traffic light changes. I raise my hand toward the taxis.

Kenny looks up the street toward Peter. "I can't leave him like this," he says. "He's wasted. And you're not."

"I never am." I try to meet his eyes but he won't let me. I wonder if he's ever seen me at all.

A taxi pulls up and I get in. "3rd Avenue and St. Mark's," I tell the driver, and don't look back.

The quick thrust of speed jostles me left and right. I press against the slick leather seat, trying to hold myself in place. I feel Tag there, in that moment. I look over, squinting to see his preppy boy haircut and wire-rimmed glasses. It's the blur of buildings, the fleeting familiarities sweeping past the window. The cab slows as Times Square fills. Tourists spinning round and round. I search the crevices between the marquees, spotting an Irish pub Tag loved. The corner where we saw Mikhail Baryshnikov buy a newspaper in the rain. The tiny window above the bodega where a seamstress performs miracles for actresses who are melting away.

The last time I heard Tag's voice was nine months ago. I was alone in my apartment and he was alone in his loft. It was three o'clock in the morning when he called, asking about my neighborhood sounds. His voice soothed me. I was drifting in and out. We fell asleep that way sometimes, two voices on two phones propped up on pillows. Ninety blocks between us.

That night, we were quiet for a long time. On the edge of a dream, Tag's voice, soft as breath, whispered, "I can't bear it anymore."

The darkness of his tone startled me wide awake and the phone slipped off my ear. I grabbed for it and it slipped again. When I got it back, I held on as tightly as I could and spoke his name into the receiver. He was gone. I called back. He didn't pick up. I threw on my clothes, ran for the door, and as my cab sliced through the length of Manhattan, I must have known, the same way I do now. The finality hanging in the air, thick as fog.

The walls I've erected in my mind, so many spaces I've worked hard to wash clean.

I will not remember our parents' death.

I will not remember Tag's lifeless body.

But I cannot forget the down of fine hair on his chest and legs, the way it tickled my skin as we moved together in the dark. I cannot forget the smell of him, the taste of him, so strange and so familiar. That, I cannot forget.

I've carried the key to Tag's loft in my pocket every day for nine months. When I step inside, there is the lingering scent of a sandalwood candle; the white walls, pristinely clean; the real estate cards stacked on the kitchen counter; the overhead lights sparkling against polished concrete floors.

I bristle, thinking of the estate lawyers' thrill when the reluctant twin no longer stands in their way to such a profitable sale.

When I get to the bathroom, I'm not afraid the way I thought I might be. I crack open the small, high window above the toilet, run my hands over the porcelain tub. It is white. So very white.

Where Tag last stood, last breathed.

I take off my shoes, my scuffed nylons, skirt, sweater, panties, bra.

I draw the bath scalding hot. Slide in without flinching. As I sink down, I think of the woman standing on the curb, her lover in some brownstone or penthouse uptown.

My skin pinkens as I look up toward the window and listen.

Music. Laughter. The clinking of glasses.

The city is alive. It flows like a river.

# THE GATHERING

It wasn't a commune and it wasn't a nudist colony; it was a seasonal naturist experiment. That's what my father said as we sat around a picture of a dozen naked people holding hands in a circle, THE GATHERING 1976 printed above them.

"It's a great opportunity," my mother said in the voice she reserved for talk of possible fortune.

I wrapped my arms around my chest, grabbed my shoulder blades through the thick cotton of my T-shirt. "They're hippies, right? How much money can they have?"

I was thirteen, and my parents were trying to make me comfortable with the idea that I would spend the next several summers of my blossoming adolescence among grown-up naked people. Naked people paying to ride our stable of horses bareback, pitching tents among the rattlesnakes and armadillos in the palmetto brush of my grandfather's thousand-acre lot. I just wanted to go to my room, close the door, and scream until my family was normal.

The planning around the kitchen table grew more intense. More specific. Potential business partners joined us for crock pot beef stew. I'd wash the dishes and listen while Mom and Dad got out the poster and talked about the marvelous opportunities. So much money to be made off those rich Yankee kids looking to spend their silver spoon inheritances getting naked and having sex under wild Florida palms.

Food concessions, entertainment, equipment rental; there was so much to do before The Gathering began.

I dodged the truth at school. I told my best friend Louise I'd be working the stables at my grandfather's ranch. Louise and I weren't popular girls. We didn't wear short skirts or flaunt our sprouting boobs at the boys. During PE we'd do our jumping jacks and wait until Coach Carson marked us "present and participating" before slipping off to sit under a shady oak and reading passages of banned books to each other, chewing on sappy pine needles. Louise wore thick black-rimmed glasses and carried flab around her middle. I was lean but not strong. My limbs were spindly thin and my shins felt like fire blazes when I tried to run more than a hundred-yard dash.

Louise had a boyfriend for a short time, a nerdy boy from band who seemed nice enough, but when she let him go under-bra and over-panties, he blabbed to half the horn section. After that, Louise swore off boys and her banned book selection got more risqué. We were in the girls' bathroom when she read to me from *Tropic of Cancer*:

"*...she flung herself on the bed, with legs spread wide apart, she cupped it with her hands and stroked it some more, murmuring all the while in that hoarse, cracked voice of hers that it was good, beautiful, a treasure, a little treasure.*"

Louise paused for effect, her eyes wide as she continued: "*And it was good, that little pussy of hers!*"

My face turned so red I had to splash cold water.

By April, the plans were set. All the vendors signed on and my parents spent long stretches of days up at the ranch getting ready. My aunt and uncle lived next door, so I stayed home and went to school. They were right there if I needed them. Making TV dinners was easy, but it got lonely, doing my homework and watching the tube late into the night. Emboldened by my independence, I declared my desire to stay home all summer. I would learn French in summer school, maybe work the keypunch for Aunt Hazel's accounting business.

No, my parents said. They needed my help at The Gathering. I would work the stables, groom and exercise the horses, ready them for rental.

"It'll be good for you," Dad said. "Fresh air. Family time."

"Maybe the naked thing isn't so crazy," Mom added. "We should give it a chance."

I cleared up one important fact. We—my parents and I—would not go nude. We were the staff. The help. We were not part of the great experiment. We just took the money and helped the guests enjoy their stay.

On the last day of school, I had to tell someone what I was about to face in the stifling humidity of June-July-August of my fourteenth year. Louise glared at my chin, just below full-on eye contact. "Can I come with you?" she asked.

I studied the edgy twitch at the corner of her mouth. "You *want* to?"

I was mortified by the thought of all that bare skin.

Yes, Louise was sure. She didn't know a thing about horses, but she'd learn.

She flat-out lied to my parents, telling them: "My folks are cool with it. I explained the whole thing, and they love it. They're old hippies themselves."

My parents were the trusting sort. They believed her without verification.

Lying made my palms sweat, but I wanted to have someone to talk to when the sights and sounds were too much to process on my own. So Louise packed a large suitcase, her parents thinking she was attending a straight-laced equestrian camp.

When we arrived, the ranch looked the same as it always had, wild oaks, palms, and uncleared palmetto brush spanning the acreage. My grandfather liked to say "The reptiles own this place. Whole state of Florida, in fact. We're the visitors to their homestead."

The entertainment tents and event areas for The Gathering had been cleared near the center of the parcel, allowing nature's shield to provide maximum privacy for the nudists. I was happy the stables were near the northeast corner of the lot, far removed from the naked spectacle. Louise, on the other hand, was annoyed.

For the first few weeks, Louise and I took care of the twenty-horse stable, working sun-up to sun-down without much of a break. We mucked the stalls, hauled large bins of feed, curried the horses in the morning. Readied them for my parents to pony down to the big tent. When the horses returned in the evening, we lapped them around the wooden corral, cooling them down. Brushed them again before bed. I went to sleep aching, a sense of peace slowly replacing my anguish. It was almost July and I hadn't seen a single naked person.

On the 3rd of July, Louise packed her suitcase and said her father was on his way to pick her up. Hard work and the lack of observed nudity wasn't the summer she'd had in mind.

"He's coming here?" I said.

"Ain't nothing for him to see but horses and snakes, is there?" Louise sat on the sofa, arms folded.

"Call him back. He doesn't know—" I said.

Mom walked in, looking suspicious. She quizzed Louise, and the truth spilled out. Before I knew it, we were in the family pick-up, driving Louise home so her father didn't have to make the long trek, and realize exactly what kind of summer camp his daughter was attending.

I tried to apologize to Louise, but for what I wasn't quite certain. She waved me off, her face tight with disappointment. I knew I'd lost my best friend, not sure there was anything I could have done to stop it. She was curious and sexual and unafraid. I could see it through her frumpy clothes and big thick glasses. And I was wound up so tightly inside myself, I needed twenty horses to care for just to sleep at night.

The ride back in the truck cab with my mom was tense. She seemed angry at first about the lies, Louise's parents not knowing about the "great experiment." Ten miles out from the ranch, her shoulders drooped, and she said, "You wanna talk?"

I shook my head, counting the roadway signs.

That night, eating chipped beef over toast, my father announced I would work the main concessions at the 4th of July fireworks. At the big tent. In the center of everything.

I dropped my fork. "Not me!"

"Yes, you," he said. "You can pour fountain sodas and fill glasses with ice, can't you?"

Mouth open, I turned sharply to my mother, unable to believe they couldn't see the problem.

"We've been through this before, dear," my mother said, in that patronizing way that made me want to scream. "We all have bodies. Different shapes. Different sizes. It's natural. Beautiful."

"Are you on drugs?" I said, standing up from the table. "Are you both insane?"

I locked myself in the bathroom. After an hour, my parents gave in. I didn't have to work the concessions at the big tent if I didn't want to. But I'd be left alone, in the cottage on the edge of the ranch, while everyone else on the entire property was under the big tent, partying.

That was fine with me.

It was probably a good idea for someone to stay with the horses anyway, my father finally agreed. With the fireworks.

My parents left the house early the next morning. Said they'd be gone until well past midnight, setting up the extra concessions, working the party, cleaning up after.

I busied myself with stable chores during the day, a lightened load since no one was riding. The music played across the pines to the southwest, growing louder as the day grew longer. Hard blasting rock and roll. Voices lost but bass and percussion carried through clearly. Looking in the direction of the tent, I saw nothing but pine trees and palmetto.

As the sun set purple-pink across the sky, I knew I was the only one other than the horses within fifty acres. I tried to imagine the spectacle underneath that big tent. All those naked people, unafraid. Watching day fall into night, I tried to imagine being older. Wilder.

I cooked grilled cheese on the stove and ate it at the kitchen table. Faces and voices swirling on the thirteen-inch black-and-white across the room. I didn't really see them, didn't really hear them.

I stretched out alone on my bed, after washing my single plate and my single fork and the small aluminum pan.

Louise wasn't so different from me. I'd kissed boys before. Or rather, let them kiss me. I'd held their hands and grown quiet when they said dirty things.

The music grew louder. It was nearly nine o'clock and the fireworks would start soon. The sky was dark enough.

When the snapping and the popping and shooting-cracking-booms began, I found the flashlight, threw on my shoes, headed down the narrow trail to the stable. I'd left the horses untied, like my father said. They would grow restless, disturbed by the fireworks. I was to let them roam free. Or they would tear the stable walls apart and injure themselves.

As I ran, I heard the horses' stirring. Whinnying and nickering.

The fireworks blasted overhead, ripping through the air like machine guns. I unlatched each stall, threw the doors wide open, and the horses bolted into the wild of the night. Galloping away, they disappeared into the dark steamy air.

They would return by morning. The outer edges of the ranch were fenced, so they couldn't wander too far. They were safer finding their own comfort under the stars, as the firecrackers continued to pop and sizzle overhead.

After all the horses were gone, I propped myself against the stable. Watched the fireworks finale, my own private window on the last moments of that independence day.

It was just me. Alone, inside my head. Why was I so afraid?

When the party noises kicked up again, I grasped my shirt and pulled it over my head, exposing my skin to the night. It's the human body, my mother said. Different shapes, different sizes. Trembling, I unhooked my bra with my right hand and let it fall to the sandy dirt below. Gaining momentum, I kicked off my shoes, tugged at my socks, shimmied out of my pants and underwear.

I stood naked next to the stable, let the air wash over me. The percussion grew louder. So I danced. Alone under the starry Florida sky, I shook and bounced and flapped myself against the night, waiting for my twenty horses to come home.

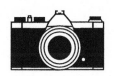

# RENDEZVOUS

I met her on a Saturday in West Hollywood at a club called Rendezvous. She was short, not quite 5'3", her hair cropped barbershop close. She told me her name was Charlie but I imagined it was Charlotte or Charlene. It was 2 a.m. She clutched my wrist and pulled me off the floor, still bouncing. We were tricks to each other, that was clear. I woke up the next morning and she was frying eggs in a cast iron pan, drinking tequila straight out of the bottle. I felt a tenderness in my chest I thought I'd lost the ability to perceive. She looked wistfully out the window, took a drag off her cigarette, sunlight bouncing from magenta bougainvillea to her stoic profile.

We didn't leave her apartment for three days. I told her my name was Rex. My driver's license said Sandra. It always would.

Charlie was a screenwriter and a short-order cook. Mid-thirties, same as me. On my fourth day crashing at her apartment, we went to Venice Beach, bought a gallon jug of lemonade, fell asleep on the sand. When I opened my eyes, she was inches from my face.

"I think I'm fired," she said.

"Me, too." Though I hadn't had a job in six months.

Back at the Rendezvous, we declared ourselves artists of the night—transcendent aesthetes—rich in the vocabulary of beauty; we danced until our limbs shook while the DJ spun a house mix wicked fast and sweat bounced between us like horizontal rain. Charlie scored more crystal off a drag queen and we carried on, until time had no meaning, until the vibe slowed to a steady trance beat and I hugged Charlie's chest from behind, bit her earlobe, and said, "Let's go."

Her eyes darted, glassy. She wanted more. I crashed in the lounge and watched her. Bouncing, jumping, pumping her fists.

More meth, more dancing. Like bumper cars and pinballs, we ricocheted off walls, flippers flapping. The lights and the beat lulled me to the edge of euphoria. Dream-like. Charlie tugged my sleeve, pulled me back to the floor with one hand, dragging a young blonde with the other. Sex-hope and adrenaline woke me. The beat kept going—hotter and faster all the time—as the blonde encircled us on the floor, spreading her energy around like candy or speed or strobe lights in a dark night sky.

The blonde was Lani, a femme top with a double-headed dildo in a Ziploc bag she carried in her red leather purse. Back at Charlie's place I sat in the corner chair, sucking a lime and nursing a beer. Lani wasted no time. Out of the bathroom, she appeared with an eight-inch bouncing latex hard-on. It was beautiful, in a slightly distasteful way, watching her feminine force fuck my sweet boyish Charlie into heaving exhaustion.

My Charlie, I thought.

The possessive pronoun I thought I'd never claim, slipping naturally under my skin.

*Mine.*

Lani spun around, forever hard.

No, I told her. Not like that.

She took it off, spread her legs in welcome.

Charlie's eyes were half-mast. I kissed her cheek, caressed her like a lover. When she drifted to sleep, I went to Lani.

I woke to my flesh burning. Charlie crouched beside me, holding the flame fast to my skin, my arms draped heavy across Lani's tits. I knocked the lighter out of Charlie's hand and slapped her hard across the face before I realized what I'd done. Lani jumped up, grabbed her clothes, and was gone. I fought off Charlie's anger with one hand, quick-trapped her in an embrace with the other.

It's okay, I told her. *It's okay.*

Charlie flailed, yelling nonsense. I cradled her, stroked her hair. Told her it was just a trick we turned together. A stupid binge after a long night at the club. The girl was gone now, not coming back.

"It's just you and me," I said.

Charlie's anger morphed into chills and sweats. I blurted the question before I could stop.

*Hospital?*

She punched me hard in the stomach. Then wiped her face with the sheet and said she was sorry.

She called me Baby, and I kissed her.

That same night I told her to put on something showy. I'd take her out for dinner to a place with cloth napkins and three forks. Charlie said she'd rather eat Vietnamese at this dive on Sunset, so we did that instead.

It wasn't fancy, but the food was slammin' and the patrons were just the right amount of freaky. I asked her to tell me about her screenplay. She got all cagey and nervous, as if I'd steal her ideas and sell them to pirates. I told her I couldn't write worth shit and I was nothing but blue-collar crew material. No creative ambition.

She told me some stories. Nothing crazy or wild like I expected. Light-hearted romantic comedy with a gender-fuck twist. Said a few studio jocks read it, gave her feedback. She would make it someday. Just a matter of time. I told her I knew that she would, and I meant it.

Charlie ate rice noodles with chopsticks like a pro. I tried to work up the nerve to tell her I thought this was more than a fling. I wanted to stay with her in L.A. for awhile. I thought I might love her.

I never said any of that. Before I knew it we were back at the club. Techno throbbing. Pulsating, each song bleeding into the next. I wanted to pull Charlie off the floor and out the door, go back to the apartment where we could nest in each other's arms until the sun rose into the full pink morning sky.

That was never going to happen.

We just kept tripping and tricking and going non-stop for days. There were moments, here and there, when I tried to slow it down. Tried to tell her we could be something else. Get clean, do a program, go to meetings. Drink coffee and meet nice women who'd survived. Club chicks who'd been where we'd been and seen what we'd seen and came out sober and awake and alive.

Let's go, she'd say. *Dance.*

Then the DJ spun the grooviest song and I got lost in the mix while my sweet boyish Charlie collapsed in the center of the dance floor at the Rendezvous in West Hollywood. The sea of our beautiful tribe parted, rushing to help, but it was too late. All too late.

That was two months ago and now I'm flying down the Pacific Coast Highway in my friend Jimmy's silver Porsche. There's a heavy sober blackness to my left, the ocean carrying things out instead of bringing them home. No lights brighten the sky. Just the sound of waves breaking against the rocks. I blink and it's 2 a.m. again at a gay disco in West Hollywood. A guy in chaps and a straw hat asks me my name and I say, "Charlie" as the electronica pumps my heartbeat faster. Six-minute segments flowing with an effortless DJ's spin, flipping and popping one tune to the next, a mystery where one song leaves off and the next begins.

# PRIOR ODDS

Callie fishes popcorn out of her beer. We're in our favorite booth at Rowley's but it's Tuesday, not Friday, and we're alone. I toss more popcorn. She sets it on her tongue, sucks it, tosses her head back. She called right after her therapy session. *Emotional*, she said. I grabbed my coat.

I slide my hand to the center of the table, near the bowl of popcorn. She inches her thumb over, brushes my wrist.

"Tuesdays are dead in here," I say. "But it beats grading mid-terms."

Callie laughs, fleeting. "How's Nina?"

"Fine," I say, as Callie's hand retreats from the center of the table.

The baritone on the intercom barks my name: "Melanie—order ready for Melanie."

I retrieve mozzarella sticks and marinara sauce in a wicker basket from the pick-up window. When I return, Callie's pouring more beer. She gazes out the window.

"Mitch in New York again?" I ask.

She nods.

Mitch is Callie's husband; he travels often.

Nina is my out-of-state lover of eight years. We tell ourselves we have a modern kind of love, that geography doesn't hinder our relationship. Of course, it does. It's creeping up on us. We both know it.

I pick up a mozzarella stick and dip it in marinara. Bite and pull, stretching melted cheese away from my teeth.

"Too hot for you," Callie says, the glimmer back in her eyes.

We've been playing this game for months. She's just curious, I tell myself. Doesn't want anything more. But I can't stop hoping I'm wrong. She lingers, and I wonder: what are the odds?

"My therapist says I should take a vacation without Mitch."

I'm tearing my napkin into tiny pieces. "Chicago's lovely this time of year," I say.

Callie stands, puts on her coat. "Walk me to my car?"

"Already?"

She flips her scarf around her neck, and nods.

Outside it feels like ten below. It's probably more like thirty, but I dig my hands into my pockets and nuzzle close to Callie as we walk. She's wearing her long black wool coat, collar folded against her neck. I have no idea why wool turns me on. I want to crawl inside, hibernate in the warmth with her.

Callie's Honda Civic is parallel-parked on the street. She offers me a ride home and I accept, mostly for the extra ten minutes I'll get with her.

She leaves the car idling when we pull up to my building, heat blowing on my feet.

"Thanks," she says.

I pull my gloves off, put my hand on top of hers on the gear shift.

"Come upstairs," I say.

"You know I can't."

I lean closer. She pulls away.

"Good night," I say, and open the door to face the cold.

My apartment is a mess. There are dishes stacked so high in the sink it has become a game of intricate balance. I grab the pack of Marlboro Lights sitting on the kitchen counter. I flip on the stereo and turn it up so I can hear it outside. I can't stand the smell of cigarettes, so I lean against the wooden rail of my balcony, looking out at the white puffy sky. I fumble with the lighter, battling against the wind and my gloved, sad hands.

Pulling shallow breaths, I watch an old blue muscle car lurch its way down Springfield. I promised my students their exams would be graded by tomorrow. I hate to see those disappointed faces when I walk in empty-handed. They'd thank me for not finishing if they knew how my head spun.

Back inside, I peel off my coat and hover near the baseboard heater for a minute, rubbing my hands together, then fall into the red leather recliner and close my eyes. I've known Callie for six years. She is the statistics department secretary and resident flirt. Raised on a farm nearby, she is sturdy and quick with a joke. Sexy because she wants to be. All the men love her. Women usually stay clear. Except for me.

My sexuality isn't something I announce with a megaphone, but I don't hide it either. The first time Nina visited me in Champaign, we ran into Callie at a pizza joint. Callie took a good look at the two of us, and after Nina was gone, she asked, "Did your lover have a nice visit?"

I nodded, and Callie winked. The first of many winks.

I'm thinking about my hand on top of Callie's as I lean back in the recliner. I should get in bed under a pile of warm blankets but I like to feel enveloped in the thick arms of the chair. I like to lean to one side and feel something touching me. I wish it was Callie's coat.

My hand drops lower.

On Friday, I sip black coffee in my office. This blank page should be the first chapter of my thesis. The statistical results are done, complete with novel applications. That all came too easily, I suppose. Now I have to write the Bayesian theory, the foundation I used to build the entire house of cards.

Bayesian statistics is a religion more than a science. The devout approach uncertainty with a reckless kind of care, representing prior beliefs with equations, probabilities. True believers know that observation alone can mislead, misdirect. Every action has a prior expectation. No beginnings without assumptions. No decisions without forethought. I have to find just the right words and examples to illustrate why no other approach to statistics, or life, makes sense.

There's a knock at my door. I jump, grateful for the interruption.

"Rowley's tonight?" It's my friend Omar.

"Yeah, sure. I'm going to finish chapter one today."

"Today, huh?" He looks at his watch. He knows I've been dawdling on it for two months. "See ya in a couple hours then. We'll celebrate."

Friday nights at Rowley's is a grad student tradition. The stats department usually has a sizable table, ten to fifteen. Callie started coming out with us six months ago, when her husband took that new job requiring so much travel. I'd always been a Rowley's regular. Now I lived for Friday nights. Callie added that extra spark: overt flirtation with the guys above the table, covert winks and footsies with me under the table. I liked to get there early to ensure I was within her reach.

When I arrive, Callie is sitting in a long booth with a pitcher of beer, several empty glasses, and the customary bowl of popcorn. I slide in across from her, reach for a single kernel of corn.

She covers her beer with her hand. "Not tonight," she says.

I eat the popcorn. "You all right?"

"You finish your chapter?"

"No."

She shakes her head as I pour myself a beer. Something's off with her.

Rowley's booths are long wooden benches and tables that seat ten. Callie and I scoot all the way to the inner wall as Omar and the others slide in. She touches my toe with hers, then laughs. The torturous part of the evening begins. We make conversation with the others.

Two hours later, Omar and a biostatistician named Nigel are sparring about double-blind medical trials and the statistical design of experiments. Callie brushes her knees against mine, turns her attention to Randy, the tall redhead next to her. He blushes every time she speaks to him.

I've had four or five glasses of beer. I've lost count and I feel dizzy. I lean over to the guys on my side of the booth, whisper my request.

"Mel's gotta pee. Everybody up!" Callie yells.

Walking to the back of the bar, I feel myself weaving. The University colors jump off the sports posters at me, orange and blue dancing spirals for my entertainment.

I take the first stall and try to stay on my feet while I lock the door. I lean my head against the toilet paper dispenser. Drifting in and out of consciousness, I hear Callie's voice.

"You okay?"

I don't answer.

"Melanie, you in there?"

"Yeah," I say. I stand up and flush, try to tuck my turtleneck back into my jeans, lose my balance, hear the thud before I feel it. When I finally get the door unlatched, Callie grabs me around the waist and my head hits her shoulder. I inhale her Dolce & Gabbana perfume and start to fall. That scent drives me crazy and she knows it. Her hands grasp my hips.

"Have you eaten today?" she asks.

I furrow my brow, try to remember. Bayesian theory. Blank pages. Eight hours straight. No time for lunch. "Popcorn?" I say.

She pushes me toward the sink and turns the water on. I know it's coming, but it still jolts me: icy cold, wet. Callie's hands on my face.

I start to slip and Callie braces me between her legs. "You need to order some food."

Another woman enters the bathroom, goes into a stall. Callie and I wait, watching each other in the mirror.

The toilet flushes and the woman comes back out, washes her hands, smiles at Callie, doesn't look at me. After the woman goes, Callie turns slightly, presses her body against my back, warm and firm.

I slip around, catch her in an embrace, and kiss her. She blocks the doorway. I kiss her again, more certain. Her arms wrap around my neck and

I slide my hands under the edge of her sweater. Her breath quickens. The dizzy orange and blue spirals return.

"I'm going to take you home," she whispers.

Her Civic is parked in the far commuter lot. My apartment is closer than that, but we head toward her car anyway. I don't argue as she opens her wool coat and welcomes me in, arm around my waist. We walk briskly against the oncoming wind. I'm looking down at my feet, focusing on one step at a time. Still dizzy, I nestle against her, trying not to falter.

I feel Callie stiffen and stop. "Shit," she says. "Mel—I'm sorry."

"What?" I look up and see a man leaning against her car. I don't recognize him at first, and then I do.

And the way he's smiling—

"I was going to tell you tonight," she says.

"Tony Lopez?" I say, pulling myself out of her coat. "Our sys-admin?"

"Hey—" Tony responds, with the lilt of a guy who thinks he's about to get even more than he was hoping for.

"What are you doing here?" Callie says to Tony, sharp and too familiar. "I told you I would see you later."

"I didn't see the point of waiting," he says, sidling up to her in that overt way I was never allowed. Or never dared to try.

She braces her hand against his chest. "Stop," she says. "I need to take her home."

"Looks like you both need a ride to me," he says.

Callie looks at me, says my name, but I turn. I'm walking away. Sobriety kicks in quickly with anger, and I grow more steady with every step. I hear their voices behind me but can't hear what they're saying. I hope she'll call my name again, or run to catch me. She doesn't.

I walk and their voices fade in the distance. It starts to snow. The drops on my face are wet and sharp, and soon I realize they're more ice than flakes.

Inside my apartment, I leave it dark. Slip a Leonard Cohen CD on the stereo, light incense and a cigarette. I sit in my recliner and smoke, inhaling full and deep. Sleet rattles on the windows.

At 4 a.m. I wake up with a lap full of ashes. "Christ," I say out loud. Try not to imagine waking in a blaze of fire.

The phone rings and I jump. Squinting at the sun pouring through the window, I answer it.

It's 10 a.m.

"Still asleep?" Nina says.

"Yeah."

"Out late?"

"Not really."

"Callie drive you home?"

Nina's not stupid. I can't seem to hide the inflection in my voice when I say Callie's name. The more I try, the more suspicious I know I sound. I grunt an affirmative response.

"I'm not going to be able to come up next weekend," Nina says. "Too much work."

Nina's a graphic designer in Houston. She is talented and driven. I miss her energy.

"I love you," I say. She reciprocates. It's reflex and muscle-memory. No feeling.

When we hang up, ashes are scattered all over my clothes, the recliner, the carpet.

I get to my office at 2 p.m., my companion an insulated mug of strong black coffee. I love the solitude of central campus on the weekends. No staff or students around to clog up the streets and corridors. Only a sprinkling of overworked grad students and faculty toil in our offices. The lifeblood of the academy.

I flip on my computer, take my coffee to the whiteboard. I'm moving on to chapter two. Screw chapter one and all that pious theory. I'm sick of it. I'll tackle the meat today. Outline the main results on the board, start filling in the details, typesetting on the computer as I go.

I follow this plan with intensity until my neck starts to cramp. I stretch, walk to the window. I've missed sunset. It's Saturday night, streetlights glowing amber, no trace of the icy precipitation left.

The undergraduate bars buzz with neon signs and wailing feedback from electric guitars. It gets a little hard to concentrate once the live music starts. I don't want to go home. I think about calling Omar, see if he's up for a movie or a beer. Instead, I turn off the lights, pull my chair near the window, prop my feet up. I watch the undergraduates promenade back and forth, in and out of the bars—couples, gangs of four, a few loners walking briskly, hugging their backpacks against their bodies.

I close my eyes and see Bayes' Theorem. Raw undergraduate emotions file into place, forming even columns of orderly histograms. Formulaic explanations appear on the horizon. Nina is smiling at me across our old messy room, begging me to quit studying and come to bed, to make love to her until dawn, then go for pancakes before sunrise.

At midnight, I walk home. I call Nina in Houston, let it ring thirty times but she doesn't answer.

Someone knocking at my front door. I run my hands through my unruly mat of hair. It's noon. Through the warping lens of the peep hole. Callie glances left to right.

My apartment is a studio. Everything is right there. The two feet of dirty dishes. The red leather recliner still littered with ashes. My bed, which is really a futon. Callie steps in and looks around.

"I wasn't expecting you," I say.

"Get dressed," she says. "I'll wait."

She walks over to the recliner, brushes off the ashes, and sits down. She's been inside my apartment only once before and I'd cleaned for a week in anticipation.

I grab some jeans and a clean sweatshirt, go into the bathroom. Wash my face, look in the mirror.

A good Bayesian faces uncertainty with a full understanding of one's prior beliefs.

Callie is not a lesbian. Callie is probably not even bisexual. She is thirty-nine and her marriage is struggling. She wants to feel something. Anything.

I brush my teeth.

Eight years with Nina. Our abstract objective of longevity: for our community more than each other at this point. The way our friends smile at us, each of their failed relationships filling our emptiness, compounding our reluctance to let go.

I grasp the side of the sink.

When I come out of the bathroom, Callie's doing the dishes.

"You're a pig," she says. "Just like Mitch."

"Don't do that," I say, laying my hand on her back.

"Tony called and Mitch answered the phone," she says. "He flipped. I had to get the hell out of there."

I move away. "Did you talk?"

"No. But he knows. I could see it in his eyes."

I put my hands in my pockets.

"Let's go to Chicago," she says. "Just the two of us."

A charge rushes through me. "You think that's a good idea?"

She folds the kitchen towel, sits down on the futon, messy with blankets and crumpled sheets. I'm two feet from her and I don't care about the prior odds. I don't care about beliefs, equations, probabilities. I want to wipe it all clean. Accept only pure observation—this moment—Callie sitting on the corner of my bed, looking up at me, her eyes full of "yes."

I inch toward her and she reaches for my hand, pulls me down. I touch her face and she touches mine and I am not a Bayesian. I lean in to kiss her and our slate is clean. Nothing has ever come before and there will be nothing after. There is only energy and flow, and the curve of Callie's naked form under mine.

Three days later, Nina calls to tell me she's in love with a petroleum engineer named Joanne. She's sorry, but it was just a matter of time. We've been saying goodbye for years, haven't we?

I call Callie. Her voice is crisp and light as she jumps over my news with hers. Mitch finally agreed to couples' therapy. She feels better about her marriage than she has in years. Things are going to work out for them. She is sure of it.

I hang up the phone, throw on a light jacket, walk to campus, slowly. I try to smoke a cigarette for warmth, but the wind prevails. In my office, I gather a stack of notebooks and printouts, slide them into my backpack. I will hibernate in my apartment, work there. Back outside, I squint into the winter sun and hear a sparrow. He's high up in a tree with no leaves. I can't see him but I know he's there.

When I get to my apartment, I sit in my recliner with a pack of cigarettes, a cold bottle of beer, and a yellow pad. I write longhand for an hour. The most lucid description of Bayesian ideals I'd ever formulated flows off the tip of my pen with ease, as smoke spirals toward the ceiling.

# TESTOSTERONE

You think I'm one of them. I'm not. I don't feel it like you do. Like they do.

Look at the bartender. Close-cropped hair, pierced eyebrow, yin/yang tattoo barely visible under the muscle tee. You'd like to take her home but she's premium grade, so you look at me. You're not from around here, probably in a hotel near the El. Hyatt? Renaissance? Back to your room after your corporate gig to change clothes, but you carry the shit you eat all day in your eyes. You're thinking about the hotel. The sheets smell nice. You steal shampoo and think yourself a rebel. When you get home to L.A., a girlfriend will pick you up at the airport. Is she hot? Would you share her with me?

You on the stool next to me, buying me a beer. You keep looking. You want to ask. Has a doctor made it official? Or am I just testosterone-injected goatee girl?

I don't go home with strangers, I tell you. Wink at the bartender, she pours me another.

I'm on the El and you sit across from me, your button-down cotton pressed and starched. Your suit jacket open, tie loosened, workday-over casual. You're reading *The Sun*, catching glimpses as you flip pages. You can't tell. I'm passing. You're digging my look. Baggy jeans, everything loose. My limbs, my jaw, my anger. I touch my facial hair. Can't let go of the fascination. Only two months into the injections.

You're staring. Cruising me, are you? I could give you a surprise you won't soon forget. Scoring a trans-man on the El. I could rock you all night and you'd never question the reality. I look up and let my eyes do that touch-and-go, the power play. Yeah, I'm into it. Take me home, brother.

The El stops and you tuck your paper under your pit and go.

At home I press the button and listen.

Emily, darling, please call me when you get this. I want to tell you what the doctor said. About your father. Please call.

Ed, this is Clyde. Call me back, dude. Got some stuff in today you might wanna see. Later.

Drinking milk out of the carton, I stare at the machine. The sound of my mother's voice. Chattanooga chewing it up but not spitting it out.

Why didn't Dr. Jensen's office call? It's tomorrow, isn't it?

I keep it dark as I undress. Stomach can't take the mirror. Not since I was twelve, before training bras and shaving cream for legs and pits and the giggling, staring, nudging of other girls.

I unwrap the bandages and the heaviness of my breasts rips through my chest, feels like knives and razors. I punch my shoulders with fists clenched, sweat caking my hair, retching pain stinging my throat. I'm only halfway. I unbutton my jeans.

Falling into bed, I stare at the ceiling fan, spinning and wobbling. Should have left with you at the bar. Slept warm in four-star linens and hammered you raw with the nine-inch realistic. But you looked soft. Like a touch-and-feel finger fuck or a tongue diver. I can't stand lesbians anymore. I'm never going there again. I'm through.

My hand grazes my body. I wish it was there to pull. The part of me that is, but isn't. Phantom throbbing. Then I think of him. The one I loved. The one who said "if only" and moved to New York. Tears sting and I punch my shoulder again. Damn girl tears. Dying to jerk off. Can't.

In the morning I call Dr. Jensen's office. Verify my appointment. Two cups of coffee and a donut at Dunkin', then I stop at the newsstand, browse muscle mags. Go to the gym. Lift, squat, lunge. Joined as Ed last week. Men's locker room smells like sweat and Chinese food shits. I want to linger, but get in and out quick, try not to look anyone in the eye, never take my shirt off.

The doctor. I hate him but I have to go. Have to convince him.

No, I don't hear voices. No, I don't see visions. I want to joke, but everything counts. Recorded and analyzed.

We talk about testosterone. Long term effects. He asks about the acne. It's clearing up. He watches my every move. I touch my fuzzy chin, thick bristles tickling my lip. I want to scream, beg for something to yank, plead for lightness of chest. I suck air and smile at him, crossing my legs.

· · ·

I know it's over. He sees right through me. He knows. Outside, I drop to my knees on the sidewalk, sobbing. People step back. Stare. They see a man. Crying. Gripping fractured pavement.

A man.

I want a beer but I won't go there. I need a ride but I walk. Five miles and six flights. In my apartment cocoon I exhale. I'm cracking. My mind is splitting open; I stare in the mirror, think I can almost see it.

Then I see him. His wide shoulders in the door frame, his slim wrist pushing a single red rose toward me.

Corny, I tell him.

He doesn't care.

He loved Emily. Wanted her to stay for the daytime. Walk together by the lake, holding hands. A straight couple. He dragged me to jewelry stores and wedding shops. It was crazy. He loved Ed. Took my fake in his mouth and begged me for it rough, from behind.

I call Clyde. Do I want a two-inch cock ring? How 'bout a vibrating double header? No, I say. Thanks, but no. Saving for the prosthesis. Custom-made. Skin tone matched near identical. Clyde says I shouldn't get so hung up on reality. Overrated. And testosterone is a bitch; it comes in waves and floods all reason. Makes you want to fight, kill, and screw all at the same time and when you can't do any of it, you want to gouge your eyes out with steak knives from the aching need. I felt better talking to Clyde. Six years of passing. Still pre-op. Not enough cash to make him whole.

It's early still. Eight p.m. in Chattanooga. Pick up the phone, hesitate. I think about my father and I want to know. Will they operate or is it too late? Has the cancer spread into his lungs as they feared? I thought I'd heard it in Mom's voice. So much denial packed in for one thing, not enough left over for the other. I dial, get her machine.

Mom. It's—it's Emily. Called about dad. Wondered. About a visit.

Phone off the cradle. My mother on the line. She was screening. There isn't much time, she says. Emily should come home. Emily should see her father one last time.

As soon as I hang up I know I won't go. Can't. I think about my father holding my hand, my first stab at roller skates. I could never get my balance, slipped and fell every time I tried. Mother gave up and went inside, said I was going to crack my skull on the sidewalk if I didn't accept that it wasn't me. I wasn't coordinated like my sister Margie—skater, dancer, parochial school star athlete. My father never compared. Except to say once that there was no comparison.

I'm at the bar again, staring at your yin/yang tattoo; I order a screwdriver and a double shot of Absolut. You ask where I've been. Why I stayed away so long. I shrug and look around. Thursday night usual. Fair share of corporate out-a-towners like the other. Looking to score a Chi-town rough chick, talk about it all year to their post-graduate educated crowd. But it's you, across the bar, who I'm working tonight. You wink under your pierced eyebrow and give me the girl-glance. The one that says hang out 'til closing.

We opt for my dump. In the bathroom, I adjust. The facial hair tells my story, but it's tough to know the score until the middle comes. Open the door and she's unbuckling, dropping pants and spreading out on her stomach, rising her hips up, offering what she hopes I want. And I do. I enter quickly. She's been there before. She bucks and I push, rock, the hormone throbbing under bone, peeling away flesh, and I can't feel anything. It's rubber and latex and not real. I'm inside but it's not me. I'm nowhere. Void. I'm dull and deadening but keep going. She cries out, coming. I withdraw and kick my knees up; she rolls over.

I can't stop the pain. My fist is clenched and I'm punching, bashing her stomach, her face, flesh into bone, ripping apart. Blood and spit and I stop. Fall to the mattress and she's on all fours, hitting back, screaming. I don't protect. Two hits and she stops. No hormone rage, she retreats.

The phone rings and I wake. My mother's sobbing; it's too late. I don't hear anything else. I hold the phone but tears won't come. They're Emily's and I don't deserve them. Emily's memories. I don't have a father.

I'm in Dr. Jensen's office. No appointment, I confess, but I need to see the doctor.

Yes, I'm sure. I'll wait.

My hands shake and I think of him. The night he proposed and I said yes and we had sex the way our parents did and we woke up to a blanketing April snow and I took his ring off and put it in his hand and said, No. It's not me. He left and never argued. Never tried to ask again.

Dr. Jensen points at the chair across the room. And I tell him. Every-

thing. I can't fake it anymore. I hear voices. I see visions.
Treat me, Doctor. Please.

# ANGLE SIDE ANGLE

Mrs. Jackson pounded the last geometry proof on the blackboard. Yellow chalk dust caked her fingertips and salted her black hair. None of the other kids cared about her theorems and postulates. I was engrossed, as always. As soon as the bell rang, though, I rushed out like everyone else, heading for my locker. I dreamed of strutting down the sidewalk slowly. Smoking a cigarette or drinking a Slurpee like the cool kids, not lugging three textbooks home for the weekend. I had a test on Monday and an essay due. I pulled out Geometry and American History, slammed the locker shut.

Such a loser.

Junior high cliques didn't have a lot of openings for a tomboyish girl who made A's and never got in trouble. I had a best friend in eighth grade who was funny and good at math, too, but she moved to Alabama with her father right after her mother "lost her mind" over a tennis pro.

Five blocks down from school, I ran full-speed across the highway, made my way to the Tropical Horizon Plaza. Strolled past the movie theater, the dry cleaners. I peered inside the Cuban deli, waved at Julio, the owner's son. Looked around for signs of his cousin, Maria. I kicked cigarette butts along the breezeway until I reached our place.

Horizon Plaza Game Center.

We just called it the Game Room.

Dad bought the place when he got laid off from the phosphate plant. It was 1980 and video games were the *next big thing*, he said. We had Space Invaders, Asteroids, pinball, foosball, and—my favorite—three beautiful green-felted pool tables. Mom complained because we didn't make enough money to hire employees, so we were there all the time. Seven days a week. Late closing every night.

No one heard me complaining.

Mom wouldn't let me play pool until I finished my homework, which is how I became a whiz at geometry. The proofs went faster if you never had to look anything up, so I knew every triangle congruence by heart.

Side-angle-side. Angle-side-angle. Side-side-side. Angle-angle-side.

"Playing pool actually *is* geometry," I said to Mom, as she wiped moon-pie crumbs off the tables in the snack area.

"Good," she said. "If we stay in business, you should have a Ph.D. in math by the time you're eighteen."

Mom never played. When I asked, she'd wave me off and disappear into the office.

"These games are for men and kids. Not middle-aged women like me," she said.

"If we stay in business long enough, maybe you'll change your mind about that," I said.

I couldn't see her behind the tinted window of the office, but I knew she was shaking her head, pursing her lips like my grandmother.

Friday night, with the jukebox blasting *Rock 'N Roll Fantasy*, I broke a rack of eight-ball and heard the cowbell behind me.

Dex wore a white T-shirt, a pack of cigarettes rolled up in one sleeve. He tugged at his amber Afro with a pick.

"Nothing in yet," I said. "Wanna play?"

He went to the wall, selected a stick.

There was a one-way mirror to the office; I couldn't see my father, but I knew he was watching Dex's every move from behind that tinted window.

Dex was nineteen, a soft-spoken guy expelled in his senior year for breaking a Coke bottle over a kid's head. He didn't have a job but he always had money, and everybody loved him. Dad said that could only mean one thing.

I thought Dad was too judgmental.

I didn't tell my parents about the little bags of Quaaludes I knew Dex carried, or the pot he said I could have whenever I wanted it.

Dex missed an easy shot in the corner pocket and I stepped up to take my turn. I felt his eyes on my ass as I slid the cue gently between my thumb and forefinger, an advanced grip I'd learned from a shark named Diaz who lived in Plant City and drove an eighteen-wheeler. I sank the three ball hard in the side pocket and Dex said, "Damn, Wendy."

I slipped by him and smiled.

My father stepped out of the office.

I called a bank shot. Made it. Chalked my cue, tapped it on the tight weave carpet. I was studying the table, planning my next sequence of shots when I heard the cowbell again. Dex's smile broadened.

Maria sauntered in slowly, like a real boy, not a pretender. She wore tight black jeans and a plaid flannel shirt. Dex greeted his friend with a handshake, a pat on the back.

She waved at me with one finger and my stomach tightened. I wanted to walk right up to her like Dex did. Cool and casual.

I stood there holding my cue, watching my father's face flatten.

Dex whispered something to her. She nodded.

"Finish it," Dex said, pointing at the table. The two of them left, headed across the parking lot toward Dex's car.

I glared at my father. Ran the rest of the balls off the table, alone.

When Dex and Maria came back, their eyes were slits and they couldn't stop laughing.

"They didn't keep her in long this time," Mom said.

Maria was sixteen and a frequent visitor to juvie hall. Five months this time, for breaking and entering, we'd heard.

Dad hung over the half-door between the office and the snack area. He took a roll of quarters out of the money drawer, tossed it to me.

"Nobody's touched Missile Command all night," he said. "Play."

I was the Game Room shill. If a game wasn't doing well, Dad sent me out to rake up a high score and gather a crowd. When I finished, everyone clamored to play.

I took the quarters and went into the main room. It was almost midnight and the place was packed. The jukebox screeched "Another Brick In the Wall" over the ding-ding-ding of pinball and the clickety-clack of billiards colliding. I sank a quarter in Missile Command and ran my fingers over the big round track ball. The problem with the shill trick was that sometimes I was too good at a game, and the crowd grew bored before I finished. Dad tried to coach me to throw games after I'd drawn a crowd but I couldn't do it. I loved to play.

Fifteen minutes I played on the same quarter. Maria appeared at my elbow.

"You're pretty hot," she said.

My face flushed. She stood so close, almost touching me. My thumb slipped off the track ball. The missiles penetrated my defenses. Loud explosions rocked out of the game's speakers.

Maria's hand fell on my right hip, slipping something into my front jeans pocket. Leaned in tight, she whispered, "From me and Dex."

I took a deep breath as she slipped away. Looking left to right, I prayed my father hadn't seen her. Prayed he wouldn't bust me and never let me out of the house again. I died quickly after that. Three lives lost in record time. My father was nowhere in sight. I felt the small plastic bag in my pocket. Two 'ludes. Maria's breath still warm on my neck.

I woke alone in the house. A note on the kitchen counter said: "Opening— call when you're ready."

In the shower, I let the hot water flow until steam filled the bathroom. I put Side B of *Dark Side of the Moon* on the stereo, lay on my bed, and stared at the Quaaludes. I'd taken one before that Dex gave me, late at night. I'd gone right to sleep and never felt anything but tired.

I put one of the pills between my teeth, closed my eyes. I could see Maria's silver rings on her dark thick fingers. The nape of her neck. I wanted to rest my lips there, feel her hand on my hip again.

I tossed my head back, swallowed the 'lude.

When the phone rang, I was still in my underwear, light filtering through the windows, soft and grey. My father's voice snapped me to attention. I tried to sound natural.

"Fifteen minutes," he said.

I pulled on jeans and a black T-shirt, threw a flannel shirt on top. Pushed my finger through a small hole in the shirt tail, watching the universe of plaid expand in my mirror. My face felt coarse, super-porous. My fingers tingled. I shook my head, ran my hands through my hair. Drank a Coke fast, did a few jumping jacks, touched my toes. Splashed water on my face.

I'm fine, I told myself. No one will know.

My father claimed to be the most observant man in the world.

In the Monte Carlo, he said, "Thought you were gonna sleep the whole day away, did you?" He blew smoke out the window, never met my eyes.

I rolled my window down, let the weighty afternoon air flow through as the sun slipped behind a billboard. I leaned my head out, stuck my tongue into the wind like our old German Shepherd used to do.

At the Game Room, I bought myself another Coke, drank it fast, tapped my fingers on the jukebox. No sign of Dex or Maria and the pool tables were full of paying customers. So I watched a bunch of jocks play

doubles foosball. I knew one of them. His name was Gar and he was shorter than me, probably not even five-two. His muscles looked like they were
ready to bust through his T-shirt, and he winked at me every time he made
a shot.

"Wanna play?" Gar asked.

"No partner," I said.

A warm hand slid across my shoulder. "Here I am."

Maria.

I stuttered, tried not to fall over.

Gar pointed to the table. "Well?"

Maria plugged quarters in, and the balls dropped. She nodded at me. I
stared at her chocolate eyes. I felt like such a freak.

Gar and his doubles partner stood there, watching. I was certain they
could tell I wanted Maria. They knew I was a dyke. Everyone could see it, as
if it were silkscreened on my T-shirt.

"Wendy—" Maria snapped her fingers in front of my face.

I took the goalie position. She was on offense. Before I could catch my
breath we were playing. The ball moved too fast. Gar took a shot. I wiggled
my men but he found the hole. Ball smacked the inside of our goal and I
jumped.

Maria put her hand on my arm. "You okay?"

I nodded. Couldn't feel my fingers.

Her smile broadened.

"You like it?" she said.

I grinned like an idiot.

She winked and I gripped the rails tighter.

I needed to sit down. But no way would I leave that foosball game.

She tapped the ball on the edge of the table. "Ready?"

"Go," I said.

I blocked three shots, captured the ball with my defender, rolled it into
striking position. Maria lifted her men to make room for my long shot. I
bent my knees, tilted my head, looked down the table. Gar's partner was a
wild goalie. He showed you a hole, then took it away. Fast. Faster. I saw it.
Took a bank shot off the far wall.

Scored.

Gar punched his partner and Maria threw her arms around my shoulder. "You're a little shark at everything in here, aren't you?"

My face grew hot.

We won the game easily. Gar blamed his partner. Said he was blitzed on Budweiser and couldn't concentrate. That made me laugh. And I couldn't stop. I held my side, laughing so hard. Maria took me by the arm, pulled me toward the front door. She opened it, and I pulled back.

"I can't," I said, looking back at the office. "I can't go out there."

"Come on," she said. "Dex is in the car. We'll go for a ride."

I didn't see my parents. I knew they were there, behind the tinted office window. If I wasted one more minute my father would come pull me away, throw Maria out, and I might never see her again.

I pushed the door open and ran with Maria to Dex's Trans Am.

Maria opened the car door and I jumped in. The windows were up and it reeked of marijuana. Maria kicked the front seat.

"Holy shit," Dex said. "Are you crazy? Her father's got a fucking .38 in the back, you know."

"Don't be a pussy, dude. It's just a little ride," Maria said.

"He's right," I said. "My dad will flip when he realizes I'm gone."

Dex and Maria exchanged glares.

Maria slid closer to me, and said, "Let's go."

Dex looked at me. "You okay with that?"

I nodded.

Dex shook his head but started the engine, pulled away slowly. Maria leaned up, said something to Dex I couldn't hear. He looked at me through the rear-view; his eyes were colder than I'd ever seen. Maria put her arm around me, gave me another 'lude. I tossed it into my mouth.

The radio was blaring Molly Hatchet and I didn't know where we were or how long we'd been gone and there was  a heavy weight on my leg. Warmth. It was Maria, rubbing the inside of my thigh. She looked at me and I looked back. I thought I might faint. Then her lips were on mine and I was fighting for air, fighting for feeling in my hands and my feet and my tongue. Fighting to feel the kiss I knew was happening, but the car was spinning and jerking, then stopped. The car door slammed and Dex was outside, lighting a cigarette. We were parked. I didn't know where. Dex jumped on the hood of the car, leaned back on the windshield, facing away from us.

"What's going on?" I said.

"Nothing," Maria said, wrapping her fingers through mine.

"What did you tell him?"

"Nothing," she said.

Her eyes were half-mast but not sleepy. I wanted her to kiss me again.

I wanted her to touch me. She read my mind and did. This time, I felt it. Her tongue slid inside my mouth, warm and certain. I kissed her back and touched her face and when she slipped her hand under my shirt, I moaned. Her fingers reached my bra. I wrapped my arms around her neck. There was a whirring in my ears.

"Breathe," she said.

Her right hand worked under my bra while her left unbuttoned my jeans. Her tongue was inside of my mouth and I thought I could die right then. There was nothing else that could ever feel as good as this.

A knock on the window.

Dex stood by the door, watching us.

"Shit," Maria said, pulling away. I started to shake and couldn't stop. My teeth chattered.

She leaned into the front, rolled down the window. "What the fuck?"

"We need to get her back," Dex said.

"Fuck off—" Maria fell against the seat.

Dex got back in, started the engine. Maria's eyes turned to flint. I buttoned my jeans and straightened my shirt. I sat upright, hoping fresh air from the open window would help. It just made me cold. I hugged myself and tried to stop the shaking. Tried to picture my father's face when I walked back in the Game Room. I caught Dex staring at me through the rear-view again.

He looked away.

Back in the Game Room parking lot, I said, "I can't go back in there."

"I'll come with you," Maria said.

Dex shut the engine off. "Mar—you're nuts."

I couldn't look Dex in the eye. He pointed to himself, then to Maria, and asked me, "Who does your old man hate worse—me or her?"

"Hey!" Maria said.

Dex lunged, grabbed Maria by the collar. "Wake up! He knows you're a dyke. And look at her—Look!—that's his daughter, you idiot. Look at her!"

I gripped the seat with both hands, wishing to God I'd never swallowed that second 'lude.

Maria stared out the window; her jaw was chiseled stone. I reached out to touch her and she froze.

"Come on," Dex said. "I'll go with you. He'll kick me out but he won't kill me."

I didn't want to leave Maria there, but Dex was right. There were some angles my parents weren't ready to see.

As I closed the door, I looked back at Maria. I wanted to apologize, to try to explain.

She wrapped her arms around her chest, and yelled, "Go!"

Inside, I told Dex he should leave. I was scared for him, too.

He took my hand and walked with me, all the way to the back.

My father stood at the office door. The veins lining his neck were thick and blue. He pointed at me, then at the office.

"You're not welcome here anymore," he said to Dex. "Don't come back."

"Dad!"

"Not a word," he said. My mother sat quietly at the desk. She wiped her eyes and looked away.

The Game Room had turned eerily still. Players holding their shots. Watching.

Dex angled away, slowly.

I went into the office.

As he left, Dex looked at me through the tinted window, knowing I could see him, though he couldn't see me. He waved goodbye with one finger.

On Monday, I aced my geometry test in record time, then stared at the palm tree fronds fluttering in the breeze outside. I thought of Maria's hands on my body, her lips pressing mine.

I raised my hand, asked Mrs. Jackson for the hall pass to the restroom. The third time I strolled past the bathroom, the hall monitor told me to go back to class or he'd send me to the principal's office. I wondered what it would take to get expelled. Wondered if a Coke bottle over the head was required, or if something less violent would do the trick.

Even as I thought it, I knew I'd never find out.

As I headed back to class, I saw someone at the end of the hall with dark hair and a slow strut.

"Maria!" I yelled, running toward her.

It was just a stoner guy, skipping class.

He nodded at me, and asked, "Got any 'ludes?"

"No," I said. "You?"

He shook his head and turned around, and the two of us headed off in opposite directions.

# ONCE IN FLORENCE, ALABAMA

I rode with the windows down, sun scorching my arm. Stopped at a state park in southern Illinois. Place was deserted. Biting into peanut butter on white bread, I scanned the nearby woods. Birds chirped busily but didn't show themselves. I grabbed my camera out of the overloaded Toyota and walked into the forest, crunching twigs with my Doc Martens. The boots were too heavy for summer, but I liked the heft they added. Enveloped by greenery, I thought of all the potential poisons: ivy, oak, rattlesnakes. I spat on the ground then glimpsed a wild purple flower near my toe. Groundcover had taken hold; no way to proceed without crushing the buds.

I brought the viewfinder to my eye, zoomed in close and shot. Capturing the purple blooms on film then crushing them with my boots. I stopped and zoomed closer to one of the blossoms until I saw nothing but a speck of white on the stigma. The air glistened around me. I'd reached a clearing and everything lightened. I turned back. Snapped a picture of the brushy exit. Capped the lens and walked back to my car.

This was an old-school road trip. Chicago to Miami traveling only the back roads. Two-laners cutting through small towns, miles of bean and corn fields, thick back woods. At Kentucky Lake, just south of Paducah, I parked near a boat ramp, headed toward a wood-plank dock. I focused my zoom lens across the lake. Nothing but grey glistening waters, and stillness. I scanned the water's edge, close to the dock, and heard a giggle. Through the zoom, two pasty white bodies scurrying behind a tree, a blanket disappearing. Teenagers, fumbling around naked under a bright blue sky.

I relaxed my grip on the camera.

Ginger had been my first. We were sixteen. She was a cheerleader, and her twin brother Henry was my best friend. All through football season, Ginger lingered in my car on Friday nights when I drove the two of them home after the game. She kept talking long after Henry'd gone inside. One night she touched my thigh, gave me a look of invitation. Two days later we had sex in her bedroom, no one else home, the door locked just in case.

The first time I tried to touch her at school, she pushed me away. It was okay in the dark, she said, but she wasn't a lesbian. She liked boys, and she wanted a normal life. She wasn't the last girl to tell me that. Somewhere after the third or fourth time, I started focusing only on the sex, which I never lacked. The girls who liked me didn't have a problem with the sex; it was loving me that disturbed them. My identity challenged theirs.

The teenagers got dressed on the shore. They embraced. The boy's arm fell to the girl's waist. She laid her head on his chest, stroked him in the sunlight. I snapped a photo. Strong composition, I hoped. Sun sparkling off the dark water. Stolen intimacy on a Tuesday afternoon.

Kentucky gave way to Tennessee and the terrain turned hilly, then mountainous. Roads winding up and down. I leaned my head toward the open car window, feeling the temperature drop.

About an hour from the Alabama border, I had to pee. Thirty more minutes of driving and nothing but single-pump gas stations and shacks for restaurants. I pulled into the parking lot of a clapboard convenience store called Downey's. A sun-weary man stood by the door, his face and grey trousers blending into the weathered storefront. He spat a brown stream of chewing tobacco as I got out of the car, gave me a cautious smile. I wore a White Sox cap and dark sunglasses, my T-shirt not loose enough to hide my breasts. I turned away from him as I walked past, felt him staring.

Inside the place reeked of sour milk and the floor was caked with dirt. The woman behind the counter looked like Grey Trousers' twin, only heavier. At least three hundred pounds.

"Restroom?" I said.

She barely looked at me, and said, "Men's room's around back."

I swallowed. "And the ladies'?"

Grey Trousers stood behind me. "Where you from, girl?"

"Charleston," I said, filling in the twang I'd tried so hard to lose.

"Plates say Illinois."

I took off my sunglasses, pushed my hat back on my head. It was more feminine than exposing my crew cut.

"Living up there now," I said. "Born and raised in Carolina."

"Ladies' room's inside," the woman said, pointing toward a door in the back.

As I walked away I became conscious of my heavy boots, the boyish swagger of my hips.

Two stalls in the bathroom: one toilet was broken, the other was occupied. I stared at myself in the mirror, fingers on my jeans zipper, feeling dislocated. Growing angrier about it as the pressure on my bladder increased.

I heard her voice before I saw her. Gravelly and raw, screaming "Fuck you, fuck you, fuck you, you grimy fucking bastard!" The girl stepped out of the stall, slammed the cell phone against the sink. She had short-short blonde hair which looked as if it had been hand-chopped with pinking shears in a hurry. She was thin and tall, yet not slight. She wore a lime green leather motorcycle jacket and had a red heart tattoo on the back of her neck. I imagined that wasn't the only one. When she caught my eye, she stopped, slipped the phone in her pocket delicately, and smiled at me. She washed her hands. As she dried them, she said, "You alone?"

"Excuse me?"

"You—where are you going? Who are you with?"

"Florida. Nobody." I said without thinking.

A strained looked came over the girl's face, as if she were solving a complex math problem.

I opened the stall door and stepped in. "Sorry. I've really got to go—"

She dropped her paper towels in the trash. Her movement was strikingly feminine though her clothes, her face, her presence, was not. She stared at me through the mirror.

After a beat, she shook her head, and said, "Jesus, I'm cracking up here. Sorry."

The stall door wouldn't close completely or lock. I had to go so bad I dropped my pants and peed, letting the door swing ajar.

The girl paced in front of the sink. When I came out she looked calmer. Her hair was damp. She'd run her wet hands through. I placed her as mid-30s, maybe younger. She wore hard times under her eyes, watery and blue.

"You okay?" I asked.

She nodded. "Can you give me a lift? Just back to the main highway. Somewhere civilized enough for a McDonald's or God help me, a Starbucks."

There was laughter, loud and male, right outside the door. The girl took her cell phone back out of her pocket, looked at it. She twitched her head quickly, and said, "Forget it. Forget I said anything."

She grabbed a backpack off the floor. It was covered in mud and dark stains. This girl wasn't local. She was a displaced city dweller like me, I was sure of it.

"Which way you headed?" I said.

She met my eyes with surprise. "No. You should get the hell out of here. You're a nice boy, I can tell. My shit is the last thing you need."

It took me a minute to register. She called me a boy in the most natural way. She wasn't mistaking my sex; we were standing in a women's restroom. She looked at me again, gave me a small, understanding smile, and her gaze deepened.

"A nice boy" in a twenty-four-year-old female body.

Not a wanna-be man. Not a damaged soul in gender crisis, as my girl-friend Barb feared.

A nice boy.

My face felt hot.

A gruff man's voice called out, "You still in there, Princess? Truck's about to roll, with or without you."

The girl hitched her bag on her shoulder.

"You running from someone?" I asked. "The guy on the phone?"

"I told you—forget it."

She walked out of the bathroom. I followed.

Two young guys in paint-splattered worker's gear stood by the coolers that held the beer, talking and laughing. A heavyset older guy at the counter held a *Playboy* and a bag of beef jerky. He met the girl's eyes. "Thought I'd lost ya, Sweetheart."

She went out the front door and didn't speak to him. I picked up my pace to follow her.

Grey Trousers yelled, "Hey! Usin' our facilities means ya buy something, girl."

I grabbed a Milky Way off the shelf, waved it at the woman behind the register, pulled my wallet out of my back pocket.

The woman moved like a tortoise and the cash register was an antique. I tapped my toe as the heavy guy with the *Playboy* followed the girl outside. I watched through the front window as he slid his arm across her shoulders. She pushed him away.

I left without getting my change.

"You said a short detour off the interstate," the girl said. "Now I have no idea where I am."

The man shrugged. "Suit yourself," he said, walking off.

The girl peeled off her jacket and sighed. Underneath she wore a white T-shirt tucked into tight blue jeans. She fumbled with her backpack, pulled out a pack of cigarettes and a lighter.

"I can give you a ride," I said. "I'll take you where you need to go."

The two painter guys came out of the store. She looked at them, back at me.

"You care if I smoke?"

I shook my head.

She hesitated, looked up and down the two-lane road, at the long stretch of nothing in either direction. She opened the passenger door of my car and jammed her things into the small space behind the seat.

"My name's Cay," she said. "With a C."

"Like an island."

"Yeah. Small sandy island. That's me."

She stretched her spine, extending her arms to the sky, as if she needed the preparation before confining herself to my car. Her movements were deliberate and fluid, with an occasional nervous twitch.

"My name's Robin," I said. "But no one calls me that."

She tapped a cigarette out of her pack, propped her ass casually against my fender. Her stare was large and questioning.

"Dean," I said. "Most people call me Dean."

"Much better. I agree."

I shifted, pulled my baseball cap off and ran my fingers through my stubbly hair.

"You had a pro do that, didn't you?"

"Maybe," I said.

She twitched her head back and forth.

"Did mine myself. Get what ya pay for, they say." She grinned.

I rearranged things in the car, and she unfolded her long torso into the passenger's seat, propped her knees against the dash.

The dense green thicket of Tennessee quickly turned into industrial Alabama. Factory smoke and smog.

She didn't talk much. She kept squeezing her battered old flip phone. Opening it, closing it. She knocked it against the window frame a few times. She was having a war with the thing. I almost told her to go ahead and call whoever it was she wanted to yell at. But I wasn't the one stopping her. She looked like she was taking a bullet every time she flipped it open.

I told her I wasn't driving the interstate. The point of my trip was to take it slow, see some things you couldn't see clearly from the fast lane. I said I'd take her to the highway or a city, if that's what she wanted.

"Just drive," she said. "Pretend like I'm not here."

That was hard to do.

I turned on my music. Old school Southern rock, mood blending with the scenery.

It was still daylight when we rolled into Florence, Alabama, a small city I'd picked out in advance as a place I could stay for the night. I pulled into a Holiday Inn and stopped. I was tired, caked with sweat, ready to stop driving for the day. "It's about an hour more to the interstate. You want me to take you?"

She looked toward the hotel.

Her phone rang. She stared at it a minute. I wasn't sure she was going to answer. Finally, she flipped it open, and said, "What?"

I got out of the car, thought I'd give her some privacy. But all the windows were down and I could hear everything she said from quite a distance.

"No" was what she said most. Over and over. "No, no, NO—" Her voice growing louder, more insistent. Then finally, "Because I don't want to be found. Because I'm not coming back."

She was silent for a long time, gripping her hair as she listened.

I went into the hotel lobby.

The desk clerk was plump and pretty. I asked if she had two rooms.

Cay was out of the car, smoking a cigarette. No sign of the cell phone. She caught my eye and came inside.

"No smoking in here," the clerk said, quickly.

Cay stepped back to the door, flicked the lit cigarette into the parking lot. When she approached again, she shot the clerk a look I hoped I'd never see again. Hatred sharp as a blade.

"Did you decide about the interstate?" I asked.

"Let's stay here," Cay said.

She stepped in front of me and leaned across the counter to the clerk. "Do you have a king room? I like a big bed."

There was something raw about the way she said it. I felt my legs go stiff.

"Two?" the clerk asked. "You wanted two rooms, right?"

"No," Cay said. "Just one room."

I looked down at my boots, and Cay slid her leg toward me. Reaching her hand behind her back, she brushed my arm, as if she'd done it a million times before. Her touch was warm and unafraid, right there in the hotel lobby in Florence, Alabama. I inched closer.

The clerk typed busily on her keyboard. "I do have a king," she said. "Second floor okay?"

"Yeah," I said. "That's great."

The room was mass-produced, basic brown and green décor. Cay went straight to the bathroom and I stood there, between the king-size bed and the mirror, not sure what to do. I'd insisted on paying for the room. Cay didn't argue and I thought maybe she didn't have any money.

The shower kicked on.

When she emerged from the bathroom her hair was wet and dark. It made her face seem paler, more delicate. She wore a large wife-beater that hung to her thighs. I tried not to stare at her smooth, bare legs, but she caught me, and smiled. She stepped toward the bed.

My duffle bag sat open. She peeked inside. "You have a girlfriend somewhere?"

"Chicago."

"You love her?"

"I don't know."

She sat down on the bed, raised an eyebrow. She had another tattoo just above her right ankle, a Chinese character.

"Love," she said.

"What?"

She stroked her tattoo. "I've never been in love. Not real true love. Maybe it's just a fantasy anyway. But this is *mine*. You know? Under my skin. Doesn't matter what else happens."

I nodded as her fingers circled the tattoo, slowly.

"Was that your boyfriend on the phone? Husband?"

She moved her hands away from her ankle. "I'm crazy, but not quite crazy enough to marry him."

"Is everything okay? I couldn't help but overhear."

"It's a game we play," she said. "He's an asshole. And I run away. He keeps getting worse. I keep getting farther. One day I'm gonna make it to California. One day I'm gonna save up and buy a goddamned plane ticket. Stop relying on the kindness of strangers to put miles between him and me."

"Is that what I am? A kind stranger?"

"Yes," she said. "I think you are the very kindest kind of stranger."

"I would have gotten you your own room."

"I know."

"Do you need money? For a bus or a train?"

She moved toward me. Took my hand in hers, brought it to her face.

"A plane ticket to California?"

"You're crazier than me," she said. She kissed the tips of each of my fingers, lightly, ending with her tongue tickling the center of my palm.

I took her face in my hands and kissed her.

The sex wasn't urgent or fast, the way I usually liked it. I never went to my bag, never pulled out equipment. She wouldn't let me. When I asked, she said she wanted to feel *me* inside of her, not something artificial. She put my fingers deep into her wet mouth. I stopped thinking after that. Stopped worrying and wondering if I was enough. Stopped trying to reach for something that wasn't there. I lost track of everything except the feel of our bare skin, sex flowing between us, natural as rain.

When I woke up, it was still and quiet. I didn't remember falling asleep, didn't hear the door, or her movement away. It was morning and the sun spilled through a crack in the curtain. I was alone.

We'd made love for hours, until exhaustion had overtaken us both. We'd stayed there, wrapped in each other's arms, content in our shared damp heat. We didn't talk. There didn't seem to be a need for words, nor any urgency.

I waited around awhile, searched the room for a note, or some other sign she might be coming back. Nothing. My wallet was in my jeans pocket, and all my money was still there. I felt like a shit as I opened it and wondered. It was untouched. I would have given her whatever she needed, if she'd asked.

I checked out of the hotel just before noon, drove around Florence, looking up and down side streets, peering into store windows. I thought about staying, about waiting at the hotel another night, hoping she'd return. But there was something about the way she'd clutched that cell phone, how she fought with it, that made me certain she was gone. Back to him.

I got back on the road and headed south. Every turn I made led to another town full of factories, the air stale and close. I searched for a park or a forest or a lake.

I found it in Gadsden. Noccalula Falls. A waterfall in central Alabama.

It took a few hours to get there, and as I drove, I imagined Cay still with me. Imagined her telling me about California. The white sand of the desert, the rocky cliffs of the coastline, months of no rain. I tried not to imagine the boyfriend on the other end of that cell phone. Or some other lonesome stranger she might hitch with on her way back.

The park was large and slightly crowded, even on a Wednesday afternoon. The plateau basin was nearly dry, the falls diluted, not like the pictures in the glossy brochure from the visitor's center. Nearly a hundred feet of falling water is impressive any day. I took out my camera, spied the falls from every angle, searching for the right light. Clouds blocked the sun. A gray hue set in.

When I put the camera down, I looked all around. No one waiting or looking for me. No one clutching a cell phone, hoping I'd call. Just the trees, a sweet city park, and falling water.

I crossed the line into Georgia. Bought a bag of peaches on the side of the road and ate them as I drove, juice running down my chin. The red clay on the shoulder made me want to stop and dig my fingers in. Just before the Florida border, I looked at the gas gauge and pulled into the next station. I restocked my cooler with water and Coke and asked the clerk if there was a decent restaurant or hotel within fifty miles.

"Tallahassee's your best bet," he said. "Thirty minutes east."

I got a room at a Quality Inn. Changed into khakis and a collar shirt, found a steak joint where I had a beer and a New York strip.

I was full, tired, and keyed up. Across the room was a short, stocky waitress with sideburns and a scowl. I nodded at her as I paid my check. She ignored me. I walked over, and said, "Can you help me out? I'm not from here. Is there a bar? Someplace friendly?"

"One," she said. "Guys mostly. Nothing worth seeing during the week."

"That's cool."

She gave me directions.

I didn't want to dance, and I didn't want to pick anyone up. I just couldn't go back to the room so soon. I could still feel Cay's body resting against mine. Could still smell her on my skin.

At the bar, three old queens played pool. There was a juke box with nothing but Patsy Cline and 70's disco. I ordered a beer, spun around on the stool, propped myself on my elbows. Watched the place like the nature channel.

I rubbed my scalp, ran my hand down my body, letting it fall between my knees.

The front door opened and a guy about forty walked in, black leather jacket over a hairy chest. In Chicago, I would have thought him pathetic. In Tallahassee, he was real.

He ordered a whiskey. Looked at me, surprised.

"It's a guy place, I know."

"Just won't get any play in here, that's all," he said.

"Not looking for it tonight."

He turned out to be a good listener. His eyes were soft and kind, and I surprised myself at how much I said. Somewhere in Georgia I'd realized how much I'd wanted to tell Cay, how much I'd wanted to get to know her. I was unnerved at how well she seemed to know me, without effort, or confusion. Then she'd left me in Alabama without a word and I was sure I'd never see her again. So, I told this random guy in the only gay bar in Tallahassee everything there was to know about my screwed-up life. Gender and sex and love and all I feared wasn't possible for someone like me.

After our beers had been empty awhile and the bartender had begun to ignore us, he leaned in close, tugged on my sleeve, and said, "Just because you screw like a guy doesn't make you one. It's just sex, right?"

"It wasn't last night," I said. "Not for me. It felt like the start of something. Something different."

His eyes were shifty and he swayed on his stool. He was drunk and I'd never felt more sober.

"You're a pretty boy," he said. "Maybe you're the kind of boy I'd like to take home after all."

I smiled, uneasy.

He was so close I could smell his sweat, his whiskey breath.

I stood up and shook his hand. "It was real nice talking with you."

He laughed and winked. "See. Now you know one kind of man you're not."

I was in bed, alone, asleep before midnight.

In the morning I decided not to stop again, except for gas, until I got to Miami. I stayed on the back roads, twisting through old Florida towns, main streets lined with moss-covered shady oaks. I drove twelve hours until I was on South Beach, sand between my toes. It was already dark and I didn't have a reservation at a resort. Didn't have friends or family to visit. I changed clothes in a public restroom on the beach, washed my face in the dirty sink. I'd picked my final destination for its club scene. The long, wild strip full of neon lights and techno vibrations. "From Boystown to South Beach—a gay pilgrimage," my friend Theo'd said. Now that I was there, I had no interest in the clubs. I lay down on the sandy beach, used my duffle as a pillow.

I'd hoped my long journey south would clear my head. Hoped I'd make some decisions, about myself, my relationship with Barb back in Chicago, my life. I couldn't think about any of that. Because when I looked out at the unlit Atlantic, the vast darkness beyond, all I could see was the face of a girl who said, "You're a nice boy."

The kindest kind.

So I closed my eyes, and remembered kissing her. Touching her with only my skin, my fingers, my mouth.

"You don't need anything else," she told me.

I believed her. The girl with love under her skin. Who I hoped would someday make it all the way to California. Where she would sit alone, too, on a soft beach, and hear waves crashing in. And maybe at the end of her long journey west, she'd remember a boy she met in Tennessee. Not a random guy she shared a room with for the night. But a nice boy she loved once in Florence, Alabama. That's what I was praying for when I pushed myself deeper into the sand, wrapped my arms around my chest, and waited.

# ACKNOWLEDGMENTS

This book has been a long time in the making and I have been blessed with many supportive friends, family, teachers, and mentors along the way. My gratitude is long and these pages are short, so I start with thanks to everyone who has played a part in my writer's journey but whose name is not listed individually. Thank you for all the words of encouragement and continual interest in my writing...After many years, I can finally say: Here it is – an actual book with my stories in it!

Thanks to the fantastic team at Split/Lip Press for believing in my work, and for making my literary dreams come true. Kristine, Caleb, Pedro, David, and Kate – thank you, thank you for your dedication, passion, and professional approach to independent publishing!

A world of thanks to my family, for your love and support, and for all the unique childhood experiences that sparked my writer's imagination and made their way into my fiction. Deepest gratitude to my mom, Cathy Reed, for being my best friend, confidante, and cheerleader, always. Hugs also to Lynn, Rick, Michelle, Oscar, Tami, Sherry, Pat, CW, Billy, and Larry. And a touch of love and remembrance to those who left us too soon: my beloved Pops, Grammy, and Aunts Mary and Mildred.

Many thanks to my fantastic teachers and mentors, from whom I've learned so much. To Terri Brown-Davidson, for helping me unearth the stories that mattered to me, and for pointing me in the direction of Zoetrope, where I found my first writing tribe. To the English Department and Creative Writing program at the University of Maryland, especially Maud Casey, Merrill Feitell, and Howard Norman, for showing me how to slow down and study the finer points in the art and craft of fiction. To Maud, in particular, for all the time and careful attention you gave to my work, and for the brilliant reading lists. And finally, this book would not exist, in the form you read it now, if not for the wildly generous spirit of

Barrett Warner. Thank you, Barrett, for striking up a conversation that made all the difference.

Thanks to the fantastic writing workshop community at the Zoetrope Virtual Studio "back in the day," including: Mary Akers, Digby Beaumont, Russell Bittner, Katrina Denza, Cama Duke, Pamela Erens, Kathy Fish, TJ Forrester, Cliff Garstang, Martin Heavisides, Patti Jazanoski, Liesl Jobson, Tim Jones-Yelvington, Len Joy, Thomas Kearnes, Miriam Kotzin, Richard Lewis, Mary Miller, Marie Shield, Lesley C. Weston, Thomas White, Joseph Young, Bonnie ZoBell, and many more.

Equally enthusiastic thanks to my University of Maryland MFA classmates, with particular gratitude to Susan Anspach, Aditya Desai, Tom Earles, Eva Freeman, Jesse Freeman, Timothy Jerome, Jackie (Orlando) Kautzer, Daniel Knowlton, Justin Lohr, Jenna Nissan, Jesse Ritz, Anna Rowser, Allison Wyss, Shanna Yetman, LiAnn Yim, and Heather Marlene Zadig. And to Lindsay Bernal, for all you do to knit the UMD writing community together.

Big thanks to my book club pals, Paula Johnson, Liz McGuirk, and Debbie Ramey, for teaching me to see fiction through the reader's perspective. I hope you like this book, and if you don't, I know you won't sugar coat your reviews!

Thank you to the journals and journal editors who published the stories in this collection first, including: *Colorado Review, Fourteen Hills, Free State Review, Happy, The MacGuffin, Mississippi Review, Outlook Springs, Per Contra, Pisgah Review, Potomac Review, Reunion: The Dallas Review, Sakura Review, South Dakota Review,* and *Whistling Shade.*

Saving the best, and most important, thanks for last...I extend my infinite gratitude to my wife, Lesley C. Weston, who started out a writer friend and ended up the heart and soul of my life. Thanks for being who you are, my love, and for seeing me for who I am. No matter where the road takes us next, my narrative arc always bends in your direction.

MARY LYNN REED is a fiction writer and mathematician. She has an MFA in Creative Writing from the University of Maryland and a PhD in Mathematics from the University of Illinois. Mary Lynn's fiction has been honored with the University of Maryland's Katherine Anne Porter Prize in Fiction, the *Per Contra* Prize for Short Fiction, and selected as one of the *WigLeaf* Top 50 Very Short Stories. Mary Lynn grew up in and around Tampa, Florida. She currently lives in western New York with her wife, the artist Lesley C. Weston, and together they co-edit the journal *MoonPark Review*. Mary Lynn is also a professor of mathematics at the Rochester Institute of Technology.

# NOW AVAILABLE FROM
# SPLIT/LIP PRESS

For more info about the press and titles,
visit us at www.splitlippress.com

Follow us on Instagram and Twitter: @splitlippress

Made in the USA
Las Vegas, NV
13 February 2023

67481507R00090